A **CANDLELIGHT ROMANCE**

D1291165

CANDLELIGHT ROMANCES

A Love
to
Remember

Ida Hills

A CANDLELIGHT ROMANCE

Published by
Dell Publishing Co., Inc.
1 Dag Hammarskjold Plaza
New York, New York 10017

ISBN: 0-440-14293-8

Printed in the United States of America

First printing—October 1980

A Love
to
Remember

CHAPTER ONE

The fog that held San Francisco Airport in silent isolation began to lift, and Wendy Devin watched the runway light reappear like sparkling jewels against a background of white chiffon. She breathed a sigh of relief; she couldn't bear more cancelled plans, more waiting. "Flight 205 for Tahiti is now ready for boarding," announced the intercom.

Wendy ran her fingers through the tumble of soft, brown curls framing her pixie face, slung the flight bag crammed with travel folders over her slender shoulder, and walked quickly to the check-in counter. She examined her papers again—passport, inoculation record, ticket, and the cards that identified her as the representative of Personal World Travel. She was proud of Mr. Vance's confidence in her ability to organize their new Pacific tours. It did much to restore her self-confidence that had been so badly shaken by events of the past week.

"Welcome aboard," greeted a smiling blonde stewardess.

It was the first time Wendy had been inside a 747. She was surprised to find a broad center section of seats in addition to the usual three down each side. It was hard to believe something so huge could fly. She had been assigned a window seat ahead of the wing, which allowed a clear view on takeoff and landing, though there would be only the ocean in between. The massive plane filled with surprising speed, and in a few minutes it was roaring down the runway. Wendy watched the twinkling lights of her beloved San Francisco disappear.

She settled back in her seat, glad the seat beside her was vacant. She usually enjoyed meeting and talking to new people, but tonight she just wanted to relax, to sort things out. She hadn't realized how tired she was. It must have been a week since she had had a good night's sleep—all the plans for the wedding had kept her occupied day and night. Wendy's thoughts shied gingerly around the word, but she was determined to think it through—the wedding, or should she say the non-wedding?

She stared out the window. A full moon touched the ocean with a ladder of moonbeams. A similar path of silver light had seemed an omen holding special promise that night she and Marvin had stood on the cliff beside the little Star of the Sea Chapel.

"I think this is where we should be married," he had said, squeezing her hand.

Wendy waited for him to go on. Though he often implied that he expected them to marry, Marvin had never directly asked her. When he said no more, Wendy answered, "I'd like that. It's such a beautiful chapel."

"What about May 25th? That would give us a three-day weekend."

Wendy started to protest that it was too sudden, but decided she was being silly. They had been going together since her last year in college, almost three years. This wasn't the proposal she had dreamed of, but she couldn't expect a scientist to be a dashing romantic. She did love Marvin—his idealism, his intense dedication to his work, the way he relied on her to handle outside distractions when he was busy with his research.

"That's only two weeks away," Wendy demurred.

"I know," Marvin replied apologetically. "But you know how I dislike long-range plans." His eyes searched her face. "Do you think it's too short a time to arrange a simple wedding?"

"No, I guess not," she said, feeling as if, while wading along the shore, a high wave had caught her before she was really ready to plunge in.

Marvin pulled her to him and kissed her, lightly at first, then more fervently. Slowly Wendy relaxed in his arms, the tension and doubt draining from her. If the words hadn't been romantic, certainly the setting was—the waves lapping rhythmically against the sand below them, the chapel silhouetted in the moonlight. Yes, she could picture herself walking down the aisle of this dollhouse church to marry the man beside her.

Wendy smiled to herself, thinking that he even looked like the man on top of a wedding cake—precise, even features; neatly trimmed dark hair; and a perfectly proportioned height, several inches taller than the bride.

The next two weeks disappeared in a blur of activity. Wendy had acquired her ability to handle details smoothly from her mother. Together they worked out the arrangements for her wedding. As her childhood dreams of scores of bridesmaids, a flowing train, and a full stage production were pared to fit the simple chapel by the sea, she began to feel how comfortable and right her new plans were. The family reception at her parents' home in nearby Monterey would be equally simple.

"Looks like we did it," Wendy declared as she placed the bouquet of pale pink dogwood on the mantel of her parents' rambling ranch-style house. She paused to watch her mother put the last sprig of lily of the valley in the old-fashioned nosegay of sweetheart roses.

"I was betting on us," her mother teased. "It's going to be a lovely wedding, dear, and a very lovely bride." Kathleen Devin smiled fondly at her daughter. A fair Irish lass she was, Kathleen thought, with merry green eyes in a small face enhanced by light-brown hair. "I do wish Marvin had come to Monterey with you tonight as he planned, instead of coming down in the morning."

Wendy's green eyes clouded. "There was an important development in one of the rice cultures he is working on and he felt it had to be transplanted tonight. He said he would be here early in the morning. The wedding isn't until noon."

Kathleen Devin shrugged in her expressive Irish way and went to put the finished bridal bouquet in the refrigerator for the night.

The next morning the first rays of sunlight filtering through the redwood trees awakened Wendy. She could hear her mother already making muffled noises in the kitchen as she attended to last-minute details and tried not to awaken the rest of the family. The ringing of the telephone cut sharply into the subdued sounds. It's Marvin, Wendy's panicked thoughts told her as she jumped out of bed and raced for the telephone.

"Wendy, my car won't start, and my best man can't leave the laboratory. What'll I do?" Marvin's voice rasped with tension.

Marvin's Volkswagen was one of the practical details of life he often neglected. "You could call a service station to start the car, but you sound upset. It might be better to have a friend bring you down, or take the bus," Wendy soothed.

"What if I can't make it in time?"

"Fortunately everyone is coming here first. We'll make whatever changes are necessary when you arrive. Just come as soon as possible." Wendy forced her voice to sound as light and encouraging as she could.

"All right, I'll do what I can. I sure wish you were here. You handle these things so much better than I do." Sounding more cheerful, he said, "Good-bye, sweet, see you soon."

Wendy painfully remembered the long wait that

had followed his promise to see her soon. She recalled her mother's tactful phone calls to the minister, organist, photographer, and the reassurance of each that the wedding could be rescheduled when the groom arrived. She thought of the awkward moment when the guests began to arrive—how each acted as if it were perfectly normal, and joined in the exchange of news, small talk, and banter that marked any gathering of the family.

As the big grandfather's clock struck twelve, the tension began to spark like static electricity. Wendy's mother passed the large trays of canapes while her father served chilled glasses of his homemade plum wine. Wendy tried to convince herself that Marvin would be on the one o'clock bus from San Francisco.

"What'll you do if he doesn't show up?" Her brother Kevin whispered the question in her ear.

"I—I don't know—I wish I had taken that trip to the South Pacific Mr. Vance offered me."

"Great place. You'd like it, especially Tahiti—warm sandy beaches, coconut palms. Do you still have the little gold palm tree I sent you?" he reminisced.

The gold charms for her bracelet and the enthusiastic letters Kevin had sent when he was flying in the Pacific had first aroused Wendy's interest in travel. She extended her arm and jangled her bracelet for his inspection. The phone rang and she raced for the privacy of the extension in her bedroom.

"Wendy, I'm afraid I can't make it today," said Marvin in the apologetic, absentminded way she had heard so often when he cancelled their plans in order to work. "Dr. Pridi of the World Food Institute arrived from Thailand unexpectedly, and I'm showing him our work. Their sponsorship could mean a big step forward for the project. We can be married next Saturday, can't we?"

Too hurt and angry to trust her voice, Wendy replaced the phone on the stand, blinked back the tears, firmed her small pointed chin, and went to face the guests. She was intercepted by her mother, who took in the situation with one shrewd glance. "Why don't you cut the cake, dear?" she asked in her most matter-of-fact way.

"Have to take the groom off first," Kevin said in the half-taunting, half-encouraging way he always used to challenge her to new adventures.

All the Irish temper that had been building up in her since morning exploded at that moment. Wendy made one quick swipe with the knife and the bride stood alone on the wedding cake.

The stunned silence which followed her action was broken by the piping voice of her nephew Mark demanding, "Can I have the first piece?" Suddenly it was just another cake. She cut a very large piece for the very small boy.

"Let's break out the champagne," Kevin called, already on his way to the refrigerator. He popped the cork and began filling glasses. There was an awkward moment as the guests looked at their champagne glasses, wondering if someone should say something.

"To Tahiti," Kevin had toasted.

"To Tahiti," Wendy had acknowledged.

I'm sure I shall like Tahiti best of all, Wendy now thought in silent gratitude to her brother. The charms jangled on her bracelet as she folded back the arm between her seat and the vacant one next to her and stretched out for the long night flight.

CHAPTER TWO

The sky was awash with red and gold, announcing the imminent sunrise, when Wendy awoke. Her watch indicated it was nine-thirty, but they had crossed four time zones and Wendy wasn't sure what time it really was. A tall blonde stewardess brought her breakfast. As she savored fresh pineapple, Wendy realized she hadn't eaten much in the past few days. Dollar pancakes, sweet and crunchy with coconut syrup and spicy crisp link sausages, were far from her usual working girl's breakfast.

When she finished, Wendy turned her attention to the window to catch the first glimpse of the islands. The towering peaks of Mooréa suddenly loomed into view as if they had just emerged from the sea. Beyond them lay the emerald green coastline of Tahiti. The coral right around the island gave it startling beauty, the sapphire blue of the sea encircling a band of turquoise where the water flowed over the coral. The two were joined by a ribbon of white water. As the plane banked for its descent, Tahiti took form before her eyes. Lush green foliage descended from jagged mountain peaks to frame narrow, white beaches.

The plane rolled to a halt before a low compound of buildings connected by open lanai sheltered by palm trees. As Wendy disembarked, the breeze felt soft and warm in spite of the early-morning hour.

"You're Wendy Devin, aren't you?" the tall blonde stewardess asked as Wendy collected her luggage from customs.

"Yes, I'm surprised you remembered."

"I'm Sue Pritchard. I had a note on my passenger list that you are with Personal World Tours. We try to take good care of our travel agents. Are you staying at the Taharaa?"

Wendy checked her reservation card. "That's what it says. The reservation was made for me at the last minute."

"Our crew bus will be picking us up to go to the Taharaa," explained the stewardess. "It's about ten miles. Would you care to join us?"

"Thanks, I'd love to."

The jitney bus followed Tahiti's main circle-island road between the palm trees flanking the beaches. The lush green was broken at intervals by brilliant red poinciana flame trees and white-flowering frangipani from which leis are made. Abruptly the bus left the beach road and turned up a steep valley. Sprawling, open-sided thatched buildings clung to a green mountainside. Behind them, a crystal stream tumbled over gurgling waterfalls into placid pools. Small cottages, secluded from each other by lush tropical growth, peeped from under towering palm trees. What a romantic setting—what a perfect place for a honeymoon, thought Wendy ruefully.

She spent the remainder of the morning wandering along the enchanted paths of the Taharaa, pausing to rest beside a gurgling waterfall, watching fish in a sparkling clear pool. She was dazzled by bright bursts of tropical flowers. In the afternoon she took the circle-island tour. Though she was anxious to become familiar with the landmarks of Tahiti and its history, Wendy found herself paying more attention to the handsome, smiling people swimming, canoeing, and fishing in the surf, or strolling barefoot along the sand in their colorful, wraparound pareu skirts.

At dinner Sue Pritchard invited Wendy to join their group. A colorful floor show followed the traditional feast of roast pig and native fruits. The long dining room vibrated to the fast rhythmic pace of the Tahitian hula, and a fire dance with flaming torches added to the drama. The native music and chants were melodious and romantic.

Wendy enjoyed the entertainment and the attentions of a young co-pilot. "Call me when you get back to San Francisco," he urged at the conclusion of the evening. But Wendy knew that their relationship was what the Polynesians call a hibiscus friendship, blooming bright and exciting for a day and folding when the day ended.

Wendy slept late the next morning. She was just finishing a leisurely breakfast at the open-air poolside café when a tall, sandy-haired American in his early thirties approached her table. He was followed by a striking brunette with a continental flair. "You're Wendy Devin?"

"Yes."

"I'm Tom Bradley," he said with a definite Texan accent, "and this is my wife, Mignette. We own the *Haape* on Mooréa. I saw your name listed representing Personal World. Some of your tours have stayed with us. We'd like to have you visit us if you have the time."

"I'd like that. I've heard nice things about the *Haape*. Won't you join me?"

"Migin and I have eaten, but I could use another cup of coffee," Tom answered.

"Your hotel is quite new, isn't it?"

"Yes, though I'm not sure hotel is the right word. We have tried to make it more a copy of a native village in natural surroundings. Club Méditerranée complains I stole the idea from them, as well as their best director," he added, indicating his wife.

"You were part of the Club Med staff?" Wendy asked.

"Yes, I came out five years ago to coordinate their entertainment and sports program," she replied.

"My wife is too modest to say she is one of the world's best woman scuba divers," Tom added proudly. "Water skiing and diving are mainstays of our program."

"I'd hardly expect anyone as chic and feminine as Mignette to be so athletic."

"Thanks for the compliment, and please call me Migin, everyone does. We brought the boat over for its annual inspection and will be going back in the morning. Would you like to join us if you don't have commitments here?"

"I can see more of Tahiti when I get back. I think a few days relaxation on *Haape* sounds like just what I need."

"Have you been down to the beach yet?" Tom asked.

"No, I thought I would go this morning."

"It's a beautiful coral beach, but the water is quite shallow on top of the reef. You have to go out a ways for it to be deep enough to swim. We are on our way to take the boat out to the floating dock this morning. Would you like to come?"

"Sounds great. I'll put on my bathing suit."

"Just bring it along. You can change in the cabin," Migin suggested.

"What a beautiful boat," Wendy exclaimed admiring the trim twenty-eight-foot cabin cruiser with HAAPE emblazoned on the rosewood hull.

"It's our one luxury. The rest of our living is very simple. But it's a workhorse too, for our guests' fishing, diving, and excursions to coral reefs and outer islands," Tom answered.

"If you will excuse me, I'll go below and get us some cold pineapple juice," said Migin as she disappeared into the cabin.

"Just make yourself at home, Wendy, while I get ready to cast off," directed Tom.

"If she's Wendy, can I play Peter Pan?" asked a rich masculine voice as its owner made a flying leap from the dock to the deck of the *Haape*.

He looks more like a Viking prince than Peter Pan, thought Wendy, assessing the tall, lean, broad-shouldered young man with wind-blown blond hair and startling blue eyes. "You're a little big for the part, but you fly very well," Wendy responded, picking up the storybook reference to her name.

"You're quite right, but not the way you meant," Tom broke in. "This is Captain Erick Randall, and he flies helicopters."

"Erick!" cried Migin with delight as she bounded up the stairs from the galley and threw her arms around the newcomer. Her hug and kiss seemed to hold more warmth than a routine French greeting.

"I thought you were in the Pentagon helping General Phillerie behind a desk," Tom broke in.

"I was, but he hated it as much as I did. The other morning we were both standing at the window watching a chopper land, and he must have read my mind. 'I can't get out of this cage, but at least I can spring you,' he told me."

"I told him I'd feel like I was deserting the ship," Erick continued, "but he said, 'Nonsense, that bright young lieutenant from the Academy can help me shuffle these papers without making them into paper airplanes behind my back, like a kid I know who dreams of flying.' So here I am."

"Where are you assigned?"

"Back to Bangkok, but I have two weeks' leave

coming, so I thought I would check on some of my old buddies before I report in."

"We're delighted you came," said Migin warmly. "We are taking Wendy out to the floating dock for a swim. Can you join us?"

"That's what I said. It looks like the script calls for a Peter Pan to go with Wendy, and I'm applying for the job."

"If the play calls for a pretty girl and flying, you're sure to be there," teased Tom. "I'll start the engine. Stand by to cast off the rope."

Tom expertly maneuvered the sleek craft between the floating buoys marking the channel through the coral. "Shall we go change?" Migin asked Wendy.

Wendy slipped into her butter-yellow bikini, regretting that she had not yet had time to acquire the tan which the color was designed to accentuate. Migin put on a French-cut, red, pareu print bikini that made Wendy feel like a little girl in her American-designed suit. Bet she doesn't wear that diving, Wendy thought, and immediately felt guilty for such a jealous impulse toward her charming hostess.

"Ah, the best of two worlds," quipped Erick as he slipped one arm around the sophisticated, bronzed French girl, and the other around Wendy, who did look like a pixie out of a fairy tale, except for her flashing green eyes, which left no doubt that she was a very real woman.

Wendy would have ducked the move had she been singled out for this attention on such slight acquaintance, but since the motion was all-encompassing, she didn't resist. The strong but gentle arm that encircled her waist seemed more playful than personal.

Two outrigger canoes were tied to the floating dock when the *Haape* anchored a few yards away. "Race you to the dock," Tom challenged Erick. The two men poised on the stern of the boat as Migin gave the signal to go. Their dives would have qualified them for a swimming meet, but during the race they looked more like two schoolboys as they splashed, cavorted, and passed each other. Tom beat Erick by half a length. "You got soft in the big city," he chided.

"Let's join them," said Migin, cutting the water with a graceful dive.

Wendy followed with a sharp, clean dive. She was an excellent swimmer, but she felt out of her class with such experts. After their swim—an odd combination of professional competence and clowning—the four climbed up on the dock to sun themselves. "Better get our fairy princess back to the boat before she becomes the Red Queen," suggested Erick, noting the pink glow on Wendy's shoulders.

"It's time we got the boat back for the inspector anyway," Tom answered.

Reluctantly Wendy swam back to the boat. It was such a beautiful place to swim—clear blue water above a mosaic of blue, pink, and turquoise coral.

Wendy stood on the deck of the *Haape* enjoying the view of Tahiti as they approached it from the sea. The great, high mass of green island with its uppermost tip shrouded in mist seemed more like a vision than a reality.

"Breathtaking isn't it?" asked Erick standing close beside her.

"Just like I always dreamed it would be," Wendy answered. "Those little thatched huts along the beach look like toys in a sandbox."

"Are you staying on the beach?"

"No, I'm at the Taharaa."

"Fraternizing with the wealthy tourists?" he jibed.

"Afraid so. It was the company's choice. They made the reservation."

"The company?"

"Wendy is a representative of Personal World Tours," Tom explained as he joined them.

"Don't tell me the *Haape* is out courting tour groups?" Erick mocked.

"Definitely not," Tom snapped. "We did contact Wendy because she was Personal World's representative. I like the atmosphere of their tours. But if she had been starchy and strictly business, we would have given her the resort brochure and gone on." Tom's tone left no doubt that it was Wendy Devin herself, not the representative of Personal World, who was their guest.

"Just checking to see if Tahitian hospitality had gone commercial since I left," said Erick.

"If it ever happens on Mooréa, I'm afraid the *Haape* will be out of business," said Migin, who had been listening to the exchange between the two men. "Would you like to go shopping while the men deliver the boat?" she asked turning to Wendy.

"Why don't you meet us for lunch at the Vaima?" invited Erick.

As the boat neared the dock at Papeete, Wendy saw an exotic jumble of wooden store buildings with Chinese signs, contemporary hotels, and French boutiques all facing the flower- and palm-lined harbor park. Shouts from the waterfront began to drift out to them in an odd blend of Tahitian and French, the two official languages. The result was a colorful explosion of people, traffic, and sea craft competing with the idyllic surroundings for attention.

"I need some material," said Migin as the two girls paused before a Chinese shop stuffed to the rafters with bright bolts of fabric in wild Tahitian pareu prints. She selected fifteen yards of bright red with white hibiscus and other tropical flowers printed on it. Wendy wondered what she planned to make with so much fabric.

Neighboring shops offered colorful Polynesian beach wear, sophisticated French imports, and exotic Chinese items of every description.

"That's what I need, a sunshade on the beach," said Wendy, indicating a woven coconut palm hat in a Tahitian handicraft store. Inside, the shelves were lined with exquisite wood carvings, polished shells, woven hats, baskets, purses, and mats. Wendy settled for the hat, knowing she would be back later for a closer look at the wood carvings.

"Are those perfumes genuine?" Wendy asked examining a display of the world's most renowned fragrances.

"Yes, I get my favorite here for the same price I would pay in Paris, since Tahiti is a French territory," answered Migin.

It was eleven-thirty and the shops began to close for their two-hour lunch break. Wendy and Migin walked through Bougainville Park ablaze with red and yellow hibiscus, white tiari, and purple bougainvillea. The brilliant shrubs were overhung by palm, feathery acacia, and flaming royal poinciana.

Tom and Erick were already seated at one of the Vaima's sidewalk tables when the girls arrived. The extensive menu Wendy received was in French. "Need any help?" Migin inquired tactfully.

"My French is pretty shaky, but I think I can manage," Wendy replied. In spite of the temptations of French cuisine, she selected a native Tahitian fruit plate. It soon arrived, looking like an offering to the sun goddess with creamy bananas, pale yellow pineapple, and deep orange papaya, mango, and tangerines.

Wendy noted that Erick's French was almost as fluent as Migin's, while Tom's somehow managed to incorporate a Texas twang. "Migin and I have to get supplies this afternoon," said Tom when lunch was finished. "Will you take Wendy back to her hotel, Erick?"

"I can take the hotel jitney," Wendy protested.

"After all I said about Tahitian hospitality?" Erick demanded with mock injury.

"We'll pick you up in the morning at seven," Tom told Wendy as she and Erick rose to leave.

"Any commitments this afternoon?" Erick asked as he and Wendy strolled down the quay.

She shook her head.

"Fine. Then I'll rent a car, and show you what a

good tour guide I could be if the army gets tired of putting up with me."

Erick insisted on a convertible, even though the only one available was old and battered. He maneuvered it expertly through the jumble of traffic and turned north on the shore road to Captain Cook's monument. There on the headland above Matavi Bay, Wendy looked down at the crescent of black coral beach and the lagoon where each of Tahiti's three discoverers had landed. "Captain Samuel Wallis came here in 1767, followed by de Bougainville and Captain Cook, each of whom thought they were the first," recited Erick like a tour guide.

Wendy's circle-island tour had visited here the day before, but standing now with Erick, it was somehow more breathtakingly beautiful, as if she too were discovering Tahiti for the first time.

The "tour de Erick," as he laughingly called it, left the shore road after that to follow a winding trail through a lush tropical valley. A small stream plunged down the volcanic rock from one pool to the next, often completely disappearing from sight in a fern grotto whose delicate greenery contrasted with the huge leaves of elephant ear.

Erick parked the rented convertible at the end of the road, where a gushing waterfall splashed into a placid pool. "Come fly with me," he invited as he helped Wendy from the car and continued to hold her hand as they climbed over the rocks marking the path to the top of the falls.

It was a steep climb. At the top Erick dropped

down on the grass and pulled Wendy down beside him. They sat in silence, listening to the splashing of the falls and the cries of tropical birds. "I can't say that I blame Tom for giving up his career in the army for a paradise like this," Erick said, breaking the long silence.

"You've known each other a long time?"

"We took our pilot training together, then went on to helicopter school, and were assigned to the same squad in Bangkok for three years. Then he came here and I was sent back to Washington."

"Did he meet Migin here?"

"Yes, she was the scuba diving instructor for Club Med. Her father is one of the divers with Jacques Cousteau. She says their family used to go diving like other families go camping or picnicking. She's fantastic underwater. That's why their place is so popular with divers."

"Does Tom dive too?"

"Yes, he and I spent every spare minute diving at Pattaya when we were in Bangkok. He's very good. I told them they should be married underwater. I was their best man. Migin said she would settle for the fern grotto on Mooréa. It was a very moving ceremony.

At the mention of a wedding, Wendy felt the tropical day become a little cooler, the idyllic setting became just trees beside a waterfall. She carefully withdrew her hand from Erick's.

The mood shattered, they scrambled back down the path, each trying to make bright conversation. On the drive back down the valley Erick pointed out various tropical plants with a knowledge that surprised Wendy.

As they entered the outskirts of Papeete, Wendy assumed the tour was over, but Erick turned inland again. This time a paved road wound up the steep incline of Signal Hill. At the crest of the hill a complicated-looking camera mounted on a tripod pointed out at the ocean as if expecting some dramatic event. As Wendy and Erick walked out to join the photographer on the point looking west toward Mooréa, the sun sank rapidly in an explosion of color that marks a Mooréan sunset. Wendy caught her breath sharply at the magic splendor of the scene. Then, almost as suddenly as it had begun, the flaming reds and burnished yellows drained from the sky behind the purple silhouette of Mooréa.

"Until now I never really believed the pictures I saw of tropical sunsets," Wendy said quietly.

"A specialty of the tour," Erick answered lightly.

"I really should be getting back to the hotel," Wendy said as they returned to the car.

In spite of Erick's teasing about it, Wendy was once again delighted by the perfection of the Taharaa's setting as they drove along its palm-studded drive. "It's been a wonderful day, Erick," she told him, laying her hand lightly on his arm.

"We have a fascinating night life tour—half price, lady," responded Erick mimicking a tourist hustler.

Wendy giggled in spite of herself.

"Pick you up at seven-thirty?" Erick urged.

Wendy hesitated, reluctant to spend so much time with a comparative stranger—although a charming one. Her own impulse, plus the whimsy of his invitation, won over caution, however. "Okay, seven-thirty," she said.

It had been a long day, but a leisurely bath and the excitement of anticipation thoroughly revived Wendy. She put on a white linen sheath, glad that the morning swim had only left a slight glow on her skin and not the flaming red she had at first feared. She had just finished brushing her hair in place when a knock sounded on her door.

"Welcome to my special island," Erick greeted her, placing a white ginger lei around her neck. He kissed her playfully, tentatively, in a way that seemed to say, "Come have fun with me—come love me, the choice is yours."

Wendy's response indicated her acceptance of the invitation to have fun, but left unanswered the question of love.

In the soft light the trees seemed more green, the sea a deeper blue. Wendy and Erick shared a feeling of relaxed harmony as they drove south along the coast road.

Erick parked at the entrance to the botanical garden. The attendant glanced at his watch, then at the smiling couple in front of him, and shrugged. Evidently closing time isn't closely observed in Tahiti, Wendy thought.

"What a gardener's dream come true!" Wendy exclaimed as the brilliant colors of hibiscus and bird of paradise dazzled her eyes and the scent of gardenia, ginger, and frangipani blended their perfumed delights; orchids and night-blooming cereus added their exotic sorcery.

"A triumph for your garden club tours," teased Erick.

"Do you promise a white ginger lei to everyone?" she countered.

"Only the ones who look like pixies with green eyes."

Leaving the garden, they followed the path to the Musée Gauguin, an open building in the Tahitian manner, similar to the natural settings the artist so often painted.

"There are only a couple of Gauguin's oils here," Erick explained. The others are in museums and private collections around the world. But there are water colors, and the initial sketches of some of his most famous works. Mostly you get the feel of the man himself and the Tahiti he loved."

"You like his work, don't you?" Wendy asked.

"Yes, I think his 'Day of the God' and some of his other paintings really capture the spirit of the Polynesian people and the color of the islands."

"I'll have to hire you for the art tour as well as the garden tour," Wendy replied.

As they entered the large pandanus and bamboo hut of the Gauguin Restaurant, the headwaiter hurried over to greet Erick with a broad smile. "Captain Randall, it's good to see you again. I have your favorite table." He led them out on the deck which extended on pilings over the ocean.

"Thank you, Timi—it's good to be back," said Erick as they were seated at a table by the low half-wall open to the panorama of the lagoon below. The flow of Erick's French as he gave their order was more rapid than Wendy could follow. She wasn't sure what to expect but was sure it would be delicious. She enjoyed being with her handsome escort who was an accepted regular, yet she also realized that he had been here many times with other girls.

"It's just perfect, Erick," said Wendy as soft twilight reflected on the water lapping over the multicolored coral below. He slid his hand gently over hers as the first star of evening began to twinkle in the sky.

The dinner exceeded Wendy's expectations—delicate fresh water shrimp, crisp salad with buttery avocados, and Tahitian lobster. Timi brought a frosty bottle of sparkling white wine which he poured with a flourish. The wine was cool and delicate with just a hint of sweetness that reminded Wendy of her father's homemade plum wine. The last occasion when her father had served his wine returned to her thoughts, but Wendy told herself resolutely, I will not let Marvin spoil this beautiful evening. She turned to Erick with a smile.

"You left me for a while there," he said gently, watching her closely.

"I'm back now," she answered gaily, and meant it.

By the time they had finished dinner, the sky was a picture book display of twinkling stars. In the light of the bright tropical moon they saw three girls with baskets on their heads walking along the beach below.

"Those are the flowers they didn't need to decorate

the tables with tonight," Erick explained. "Watch the girls toss them into the ocean to appease the Gods for having picked them."

"Let's go down with them and walk on the beach," Wendy said impulsively. In seconds the two Americans, who had been dining elegantly on French cuisine, became truant schoolchildren wading along the water's edge, shoes in hand. The kisses they exchanged were light and gay, avoiding deep emotion.

When Wendy returned to her hotel that night, she scarcely felt her feet touch the floor and was oblivious to the sand she was trailing behind her. "Letter for you, miss," said the clerk handing her a small, heavy envelope along with her key.

Wendy was surprised to see the address in Marvin's hasty scrawl. Dropping the letter in her purse, she hurried to her room, her heels sharply ringing along the stones of the path.

With the door firmly closed behind her, Wendy took the letter from her purse and stared at it for a long moment. She was tempted to drop it unopened into the wastebasket, but as she tapped it against her fingers in indecision, she felt a heavy metal object in the envelope. Curiosity triumphed, and she ripped the envelope open impatiently; out slid a small gold object—a forget-me-not for a charm bracelet.

Wendy examined the exquisite detail of the small gold flower she held in her hand. It must have taken a determined search to find such a fine piece of work. Wendy could imagine the effort it cost Marvin, who hated shopping. In spite of herself, an understanding smile crept across her face as she pictured him on such a quest. She removed a small, neatly printed card from the envelope and read:

"Joy to forgive and joy to be forgiven
Hang level in the balance of Love."

Marvin

CHAPTER THREE

Wendy was waiting in the lobby the following morning when Tom and Migin arrived. What a handsome couple, she thought as she watched the tall, ruggedly masculine Texan and his vivacious French wife.

"How's our favorite travel agent?" Tom greeted her. He hesitated, as if remembering Erick's barbs about promoting their resort.

"Wendy, we're so glad you can come," Migin tactfully added.

"I'm looking forward to it," Wendy replied warmly as Tom loaded her suitcase into the back of the taxi.

With the morning sun striking its gleaming bow, the *Haape* seemed even more inviting. "Ready to go battle Captain Hook and the pirates?" asked Erick as his head emerged from the galley.

Wendy laughed at this reference to Peter Pan and

Wendy, although the joke had always annoyed her when she was younger. With Mooréa looming before them, a purple shape on a background of azure sea and sky, the world of fairy tales did not seem so far-fetched.

As the *Haape* approached Mooréa, the purple turned deep green, the landscape more lush than Tahiti with sharper, more jagged mountains. With an ease which belied the difficulty of the task, Tom maneuvered the *Haape* through the pass in the barrier reef, across the colorful coral, and into the blue lagoon.

"That's the Bali Hai," said Erick pointing to a collection of huts set on pilings constructed out over the water. Bronzed figures swam in the lagoon or lazed on the white sand beach.

"Watch the tallest mountain on the left, and see if the Gods of Mooréa welcome you," Erick instructed.

As Wendy watched, the clouds covering the peak he had indicated began to lift. In the top of the mountain was a round hole as if a cannon had been shot through it. "That's the Eye of the Gods that watch over Mooréa come out to take a look and bid you welcome," he told her.

Adding their own welcome, two native boys in an outrigger canoe, a small copy of the war canoes which originally brought their ancestors to the islands, paddled alongside and shouted greetings. At the end of the bay Tom docked the boat beside a number of outrigger canoes. When Wendy stepped onto the dock she noticed the open-sided, native style huts hidden among the palms. "*Haape* landing," quipped Erick.

Migin led Wendy to a pandanus and bamboo hut raised off the ground on coconut-trunk stilts. Split log steps led up to a small open-faced porch, with bamboo shutters swung upward to the eaves in place of windows. A woven straw mat on the floor blended with the natural materials of the walls and thatched roof. A red-and-white pareu print covered the bed and divided the tiny bath from the rest of the room. Now Wendy knew why Migin had bought all the pareu print when they were shopping in Papeete.

"It's just perfect, Migin," said Wendy.

"We think people want to experience Mooréa as it really is," answered Migin. "Tom will bring up your suitcase when he gets the supplies unloaded. I'll be down in the main compound."

Erick came bounding up the path a few minutes later, swinging her suitcase like a small boy's book satchel. Wendy hoped that a suitcase which had come as far as hers could be trusted not to fly open.

"What do you think of it?" he asked.

"It's like a travel poster of the South Pacific come to life."

"We aim to please," he answered as if he had conjured up the entire setting himself. "Shall we explore?"

He led her along the beach, past several similar huts hidden in the trees. "Need any help?" he called to Migin as they passed the open-sided dining hall. Long tables and benches set around a square platform looked like a combination scout camp mess hall and a makeshift nightclub.

"No thanks, the boys have things so well organized they could really run the place without us," Migin answered, nodding to the Polynesian boys preparing the room for lunch.

The beach was a narrow ribbon of white sand between the coral-patterned blue lagoon and the lush tropical foliage. The warm sun on the sand had enticed small, brown land crabs out of their hiding places. Wendy and Erick passed hundreds of their holes. When Erick came close to one, he scampered after it, trying to outrace it before the small creature could vanish into its hole. Finally, running full speed, he cornered one between two rocks. The crab put up both claws like a fighter in the ring and snapped at anything within reach.

"I told you we would battle Captain Hook and his men," Erick said as the small crab cut cleanly through the twigs he offered.

"I got heem," shouted a young voice as a small brown hand shot out between the rocks, grasping the crab just behind the claws.

Wendy and Erick had been so engrossed with the crab that they had not noticed the small native boy slip out through the trees. He held a long bamboo pole with palm leaves tied to one end with a string. He took the crab to a reed basket up the beach. "I'm Tautu," the boy introduced himself, holding out a bronzed hand after first wiping it on his ragged shorts.

"What do you have there?" Erick asked indicating the bamboo pole.

"That's a crab pole," Tautu said, casting the bunch of leaves into one of the crab holes. He jiggled the bait slightly until the pole began to bend like a fishing rod with a catch. He whipped the pole into the air with a crab dangling from it by one claw entangled in the palm leaves. The crab let go and plopped at the boy's feet, another addition for the bamboo basket.

"You want to try?" he asked passing the pole to Erick. Erick made three attempts but failed to bring a crab out of its hole. "You gotta wait until he has a tight hold," the boy instructed. Erick's next attempt was successful.

Wendy watched as Erick and Tautu passed the pole back and forth, alternating catches like Tom Sawyer and Huckleberry Finn or Peter Pan and the Lost Boys.

"I got enough for bait, and Dad's waiting to go fishing," Tautu told them when he and Erick had landed about a dozen. He picked up the basket and jogged up the beach, pausing to wave before he disappeared into the palm trees.

Erick returned the boy's signal. "I guess it's time we got back to our *Haape* home for lunch."

She wrinkled a lightly freckled nose at his play on words, and hand-in-hand they turned back down the beach. As they came within sight of the first hut, a blast sounded on the conch horn. By the time they reached the open-air dining hall, the other guests were already seated. There were two dozen people, mostly young, an equal number of men and women. The snatches of conversation which reached Wendy as they entered were mostly in French with a sprinkling of English and German.

From one end of a long table Migin beckoned them to join her. As she stepped lightly over the bench and sat down, Wendy realized how hungry she was. The table had a hibiscus in the center, flanked by pineapple boats filled with tropical fruit. Polynesian boys served steaming plates of rice and small freshwater shrimp in a rich sauce.

"A perfect blend," Wendy told Migin, enjoying the mixture of French cuisine and native delicacies.

"Tonight will be the real feast," Migin replied. "We have been invited to Club Med for a *tamaaraa*, a native feast. Each resort on Mooréa takes a turn at hosting the feast and invites all the guests on the island. Actually the feast is prepared by the Mooréans; we just furnish the food.

"Sounds like fun."

Wendy was glad she had taken the time to buy a pareu in Tahiti. The salesgirl had called the native wraparound of white with red flowers instead of the usual red with white flowers a reverse print. The white made a glowing bronze of Wendy's newly acquired tan.

Tom drove the microbus, since the boy who usually drove had gone ahead to help prepare the feast. The bus followed the graveled circle-island road along the white sandy beach. Lush tropical growth reached down to the road and sometimes arched over it. As the sun sank in the sky, the bright coral of the ocean bottom began to develop colorful shadow patterns. The road was deserted.

The thatched huts of Club Mediterranée were A-frame rather than the open-sided Tahitian design. There were nearly a hundred of them scattered in the trees around the central compound. Marked white-rock trails led from one area to another.

Erick and Wendy followed one that led to the beach, where the setting sun made a blazing path across the water.

"I crown you Sunset Island Princess," said Erick, placing a flower *couronnes* he had coaxed from one of the native girls on Wendy's head. He kissed her on each cheek, his arms slipping from her shoulders to her waist, pulling her to him. As he kissed her tenderly, Wendy did indeed feel like the princess of an enchanted isle.

Erick released her reluctantly. The agelessness of sea and sand imparted a timeless quality to their short friendship, and the magic of the tropical twilight needed no words. . . .

"Eeerek!" cried a tall blonde girl dashing up behind him. As he turned, she flung her arms around him and smothered him with a kiss. "Migin didn't tell me you were coming."

"They didn't know I was. I didn't know myself until the last minute."

"With you things are always quite sudden," she said accusingly.

"Dominique Maraux, this is Wendy Devin," Erick replied with belated introductions.

"Bonjour," the French girl nodded, eyeing Wendy appraisingly.

"Wendy is with Personal World Travel," Erick added.

Wendy felt vaguely insulted by his apparent need to explain her presence, and found it difficult to keep the chill out of her voice as she acknowledged the introduction.

"You're looking well, Niki," Erick said, regarding the shapely girl in her halter-topped native costume.

"And you are dashing as usual," she returned. "Are you staying long?"

"Only a few days. I have to be back in Bangkok in a week."

At the mention of Bangkok a shadow crossed the girl's smiling face, but it was gone so quickly that Wendy wondered if she had just imagined it.

"It looks as if our painted South Seas sunset has vanished. Shall we join the others?" Erick asked as he slipped an arm around each girl and started back up the beach.

There was a long blast on the conch shell and everyone gathered around the *ahimaa*, the earth oven. A Mooréan boy scraped the steaming lava rocks from the top with a shovel. When the oven was open, four men lifted out a leaf-wrapped pig which had been roasting on a spit inside. Two boys dipped their hands into a bucket of cold water and, reaching inside the roast pig, tossed out smoldering lava rocks. The pig was carved with ceremony and generous slices were placed on the guests' plates, which were then piled high with baked yams, taro, baked wild banana, breadfruit, and coconut.

Wendy, Niki, and Erick joined Migin and Tom at one of the long tables in the dining hall—a building several times larger than the *Haape*'s but of the same open-sided design. While the others reminisced about their past times together, Wendy wished she felt less of an intruder. Any attempt to leave would be more embarrassing than just sitting, smiling, and commenting politely whenever Erick turned to include her in the conversation.

"Did Migin tell you Dad and Uncle Maurice are coming out Saturday? They want to do some diving off Bora Bora. A postman's holiday they call it. We will be diving with them. Won't you join us?" Niki asked Erick.

He hesitated, and she added, "You met Uncle Maurice, Migin's father, at the wedding. He's fun to dive with."

"I'm afraid I would be way out of my class," Erick answered.

"Nonsense. We'll just be diving for fun and to look for new species of fish. It takes more luck than anything else for that. We'd love to have you," she pleaded.

"Dad always says the more eyes looking the better chance of spotting something," Migin added.

"It's not often an amateur has the opportunity to dive with the Cousteau divers, even when they are on vacation," Erick acknowledged.

The soft strum of guitars brought an end to conversation. The tempo became faster, more insistent, and three girls in grass skirts and flower leis began gyrating in the vigorous, sensuous Tahitian hula. Their exuberance was matched by men with flaming torches in the fire dance, and by a sword dance of combat with bamboo poles, all done to the ritual of ancient chants. The performances were less polished than those in Tahiti, but more spontaneous and enthusiastic. The dances became group affairs with most of the natives and some of the guests joining in.

"Come on, Erick. I'm sure you still remember how," urged Niki, taking him by the hand.

They were quite a striking contrast, the tall blond couple almost a head taller than the native dancers. Niki moved with natural grace and rhythm, and after a few tentative steps, Erick picked up the beat.

"Aren't they beautiful?" Wendy said turning to Migin, who had moved beside her when Niki and Erick left. "Did she say she's your cousin?"

"Not really. We grew up in the same town. Our fathers both dive for Jacques Cousteau. That's why she calls my father Uncle Maurice. We came out to Mooréa together to direct Club Med's diving program. She was maid of honor at my wedding."

"And is that where she met Erick?"

"Yes, and she fell madly in love with him. Of course Niki is always falling madly in love, but Erick was different."

"What happened?"

"There was a girl back in Bangkok. Neither Tom nor Erick ever talk much about it."

The throbbing drums stopped abruptly. Niki and Erick returned to the table breathless and laughing. "What's the matter, you getting too old for native dancing?" Erick asked Tom.

"I always figured dying and dancing should be done with your boots on," answered Tom in an exaggerated drawl.

"Do you ever call him Tex instead of Tom?" Wendy asked Migin.

"It's a temptation I fight with great willpower," confessed Migin affectionately.

The guitars began to strum the haunting strains of "Aloha" and the guests started to leave. The regular driver was already in the microbus when they arrived. Tom and Migin took the seat behind him, and Wendy the one by the window across from them. She saw Erick brush Niki's cheek lightly with a kiss, then come bounding up the steps as she called after him, "Don't forget Saturday."

It was a quiet ride back to the *Haape* through the starlit tropical night. Soon the hum of the motor began to blend with the lapping of the waves, and Wendy's head dropped lightly onto Erick's shoulder.

She awoke with a start, somewhat embarrassed as the bus rocked to a stop in the *Haape*'s main compound. Erick took her hand to help her down the steps of the bus and held it as they walked along the beach to her cabin. When they reached her porch, he raised her hand to his lips and kissed it in the continental manner. Then he turned abruptly and vaulted down the steps. "Tomorrow we go native," he called back over his shoulder as he disappeared into the shadows.

Wendy stood a moment, thoroughly confused and shaken by the evening and its abrupt ending. Shrugging, she went into her hut to get ready for bed.

The cries of myna birds awakened Wendy to the crisp freshness of the tropical morning. She lay still for several minutes, listening to the exotic sounds of the birds greeting the day. What do you wear to go native, she wondered. In these islands going native must involve the water, she decided, so she put on her butter-yellow bikini. This time the contrast with her bronzed skin gave the effect she had hoped for when buying it. She slipped on the matching painter's smock over the top, wishing the smock didn't make her look so much like a little girl.

As Wendy stepped quietly out her door she saw Erick sitting on the beach a few yards away, completely absorbed in the sea and sky. He did not hear her approach until she sat down beside him. "I was hoping you would be up early," he said, smiling his approval. "Let's get a bite to eat in the kitchen and we can get started."

"Want me to fix some sandwiches?" the cook offered when they had finished breakfast.

"No thanks, we're going native," Erick answered.

Erick led her to one of the small outrigger canoes, helped her into the bow, and handed her a paddle. "Even an island princess has to paddle her own canoe," he told Wendy as he picked up the other paddle and shoved the canoe away from the dock.

It had been several years since she had gone canoeing, but Wendy was grateful she had learned to paddle at scout camp. She bit the blade of the paddle into the water in a long sweeping motion.

"You *are* a native princess," said Erick approvingly.

"Just a well-trained Girl Scout," she answered honestly, hoping she didn't look too much like one.

Erick guided the canoe out of the bay and into the Opunohu River. The stream was so overhung with branches and trailing vines that they might have been in an African jungle. Paddling slowly, they passed a continual parade of floating red and yellow pareu blossoms—a giant lei on a broken string.

"It is so beautiful, I think you conjured it up," said Wendy as they paused to enjoy the solitude and splendor of the river.

"A fairy tale needs a wonderland setting," Erick replied. With wordless accord they began paddling again. After a while, the sound of birds in the trees was replaced by an increasing roar. The canoe broke into a clearing where the river tumbled over a lava cliff into a deep pool. They beached the canoe on the black lava sand.

"Last one in is a sissy," Erick called as he began peeling off his shirt and dashing into the clear blue water. With a quick zip Wendy was out of her smock and into the water ahead of him.

"That's not fair—shirts don't have zippers," he complained in mock indignation.

After the salt water of the lagoon, the pool felt clean and refreshing. They splashed and dived like dolphins at play. When they had finished their swim and lay in the sun to dry, Wendy was surprised to find the black sand was as smooth and comfortable as the best white sand beach. She was almost asleep when Erick announced. "Time to start lunch."

He took a coil of fish line and a hook from his shirt pocket. A few minutes' search produced a large caterpillar for bait. Climbing onto a large boulder beside the falls, he dropped the line over the edge. He didn't have to wait long before there was a tug on the line; a deft flip landed his catch. The second bite flipped off the hook halfway out of the water, but a third try was again successful.

They quickly gathered enough dry wood for a small fire on the beach and Erick surprised Wendy by expertly gutting and scaling the fish. "But I failed the course in stick rubbing," he quipped, producing matches from his shirt pocket to light the fire. "While that burns down to coals, we'll get the rest of our dinner," he said, starting along a dim path through the underbrush. The path led to breadfruit and mango trees.

"Nature's delicatessen," said Wendy as they filled their arms.

"Now for the final touch," Erick announced as they deposited their treasures beside the small beach fire. He went to a spot where the stream entering the clearing had undercut the bank. A coconut palm leaned out over the water at a sharp angle. Walking up the trunk monkey fashion, he tossed down drinking nuts.

"Just right," was Erick's verdict on the coals when they returned to the fire. He skewered the flattened fish on sharpened sticks which they held over the glowing coals. "Survival training was never like this," he mumbled between bites of broiled fish and breadfruit.

"Neither was scout camp," agreed Wendy, wiping the mango which dripped down her chin.

"Now you get your nap," Erick told her as he finished burying the last telltale signs of their meal and sprawled lazily on the sand. Wendy stretched luxuriously in the sun, determined not to doze off as she had on the bus the night before but the early start, the morning's activity, and the rich lunch made sleep irresistible. . . .

Wendy awakened to the light touch of Erick's lips brushing hers. "Only way to wake a sleeping beauty," he said, kissing her again more fervently.

Wendy longed to return Erick's kiss with equal ardor, but her feelings were complicated by thoughts of the glamorous Niki and a mysterious girl in Bangkok. Erick moved abruptly away from her, and she realized that her sudden chill came from a menacing dark cloud blotting out the clearing overhead.

"Have to make a dash for it," Erick said, pulling her toward the canoe so fast that her feet scarcely touched the ground. Just as they reached the canoe, the rain hit, driven by such fierce wind that it struck their faces like hail. Erick turned abruptly and pulled Wendy back along the beach as the rain now pelted down against their backs.

At the edge of the falls behind the rock from which Erick had fished there was a deep crevass slightly taller than Wendy. Crouching, Erick ducked through the opening with Wendy close at his heels. Behind the rock was a wind-hollowed cave the size of a child's playhouse, protected from the driving rain by the large rock which almost blocked the entrance. As they peered out of the narrow opening, the rain began to come down in almost solid sheets. Instinctively they huddled close together as Erick slipped a protective arm around her, his playful manner of a few minutes ago gone now. It was an oddly satisfying experience to huddle in that small, private world while the storm raged about them. The roar of wind and water made conversation impossible, but the communication between them was complete. Wendy had never known such a sense of peace and contentment.

The storm and the enchanted moments that accompanied it ended as abruptly as they had begun. The violent tropical storm turned to a slow drizzle.

"A *marazmu*, the cold wind and rain that sweeps down from the north several times each year," Erick explained. "It will probably rain all day. Tom and Migin may be concerned about us, so I think we should start back."

They walked hand-in-hand down the beach. Already soaked through, they did not hurry. "Since we'll be going downstream, just use your paddle to steer and hold the front as straight as possible," Erick instructed, as he helped Wendy into the canoe and shoved it away from shore. It glided rapidly over the churning red-brown water. At several points, small tumbling streams rushed to join the river. At such places, Wendy was able to keep the bow of the canoe pointed downriver by a series of short, sharp strokes against the current. With each additional stream, the river rushed faster and roared louder.

Suddenly Wendy heard Erick's voice above the rumbling water, but she was unable to distinguish his words. Looking back quickly, she saw him signal toward the shore. At the same moment, the surging water twisted the canoe with a rough jolt. Wendy worked furiously to hold the bow of the canoe against the spiraling current, but it was too strong for her. She felt the struggle being waged between the whirling water and the man seeking to control the fragile craft. Finally the man won, and the canoe swung toward shore. Wendy paddled rapidly with short, biting motions, feeling the thrust of Erick's powerful strokes. As the bow of the canoe touched the bank, Erick leapt out and pushed the front onto shore. Wendy jumped out lightly after him and helped him drag the canoe out of the water.

Erick stood motionless, staring at the tremendous rush of water and the small, shivering girl beside the fragile boat. As if determined to protect Wendy from the water, the rain, or any other force, he gathered her in his arms and kissed her possessively, then slowly released her.

"We'll walk from here. The boys will come for the canoe when the storm is over."

The thick growth formed an umbrella over them, but whenever they had to push the undergrowth aside, it released a shower of trapped water. When they finally emerged onto the beach where they had chased land crabs the first day, the sea was running so high that the spray dashed against their legs. It would have made short work of a canoe.

"Alo!" shouted Ruanu the cook as they came in sight of the cabins.

Migin came racing down the beach and threw her arms around Erick and then Wendy. "We were afraid you were marooned on one of the little coconut islands. Tom and some of the boys are out in the boat looking for you."

"We went up the river, but the current was too strong to bring the canoe out into the lagoon, so we beached it and walked across above the delta," Erick told her.

"Go radio Tom," Migin directed Ruanu. "Wendy, you're drenched and shivering. Go get a hot bath and hop into bed and Ruanu will bring you up something warm," Migin ordered.

As she headed for her cabin, Wendy giggled at the thought of Migin's chicken-soup-mothering on a Pacific hideaway. She had scarcely finished the prescribed shower and settled into bed with a blanket around her Indian fashion when there was a knock at the door. Migin entered, followed by Erick, who was carrying a covered bowl from which spiraled wisps of steam. He set the bowl on the table beside her bed. Wendy lifted the cover—it was fish chowder, not chicken soup.

"Bouillabaisse we called it at home," said Migin. "Ruanu starts a big pot whenever a norther blows up."

"It looks marvelous—shrimp, crab, mahi mahi, and some things I'm sure I've never seen before."

"Probably not," said Erick. "There are some very unusual and beautiful fish here. You'll have to get acquainted with them on the first sunny day." He gazed at her fondly.

A bit chagrined at the bedraggled ending to her romantic escapade, Wendy nevertheless smiled up at her two friends.

"Thanks so much for everything," she said. "I feel fine now."

Erick bent over to kiss her on the forehead and, despite her exotic adventures, she felt like a little girl again.

* * *

The next morning Wendy was again awakened by the myna bird greeting the sun. The rain had stopped in the night, but water still dripped from the trees. As she raised the shutter to the warm sunlight, Wendy saw Erick sitting on the beach where he had been the previous morning. It would be perfect to spend endless days playing in the sun, sand, and sea, but Wendy knew this must be the last day for her. She reminded herself sternly that this was a business trip, not a vacation.

"Hi, ready to go meet the fish?" Erick greeted as she sat down on the sand beside him.

"I'm afraid I'm going to have to snub the fish and go back to work."

"Have you told Migin?"

"No. They're so busy with their other guests that I hate for them to have to take me back. Is there a public boat or plane I can take?"

"Yes, you can get either one from Temae in the afternoon. Where will you go next?"

"Bali."

"I like Bali. Where will you be staying?"

"Tandjung Sari. It's Balinese style."

Later, Migin, joined them for breakfast. "Do you really have to go?" she protested.

"Business before pleasure, I'm afraid, though I have already made up my mind which area I want to represent," answered Wendy. "Your beautiful Pacific Islands have completely captivated me."

"It's our super-salesman who does it," said Tom, turning to Erick with a mischievous grin.

"I'll take the afternoon plane," said Wendy, cutting short Tom's offer to take her back to Tahiti.

"Then you'll still have time to meet my friends the fish," interposed Erick.

When breakfast was finished, the four friends took the cruiser down the now glassy-calm bay and anchored just beyond the coral reef. Erick helped Wendy put on fins. She flapped across the deck feeling like a circus clown in great floppy shoes. He adjusted a face mask over her eyes and nose, pulling it tight enough to prevent seepage, and showed her how to breathe through the snorkel. At first Wendy felt a brief moment of panic with her eyes and nose confined in the glass enclosure, but she adjusted quickly.

Wendy and Erick slipped over the side of the boat and clung to it for a moment. Then Erick floated facedown on top of the water. Wendy pushed off from the side of the boat in a long smooth glide, but became confused about breathing through her mouth and surfaced, spluttering and coughing.

"Breathe only through the mouthpiece," Erick told her, flipping her mask up on top of her head.

Tom and Migin were gliding smoothly over the surface of the water, intent on the underwater view. Wendy replaced her mask, determined to try again. This time she started more slowly with a few gentle flutters of her feet as she led with her hands to keep from running into anything. The view was breathtaking. The coral beneath them was clearly visible in colors of blue, pink, yellow, white, and red. Fish looking like creations of a modern artist began to swim past—black, white, and yellow striped ones, and red, green, blue, and pink ones. Erick took Wendy's hand and they floated side by side as he pointed out some of the shyer creatures peering from holes or flattening themselves against the rocks like colorful flowers.

Wendy had originally thought that going snorkeling would be an odd way to spend their last day together, but floating through this undersea wonderland now seemed a fitting conclusion to her brief but joyous interlude with Erick.

CHAPTER FOUR

The sun was just tinging the blue waters of the Pacific with a rosy glow as the plane circled for its landing on Bali. Wendy wondered whether flights to South Sea islands were scheduled to arrive at sunrise because it made the flight routine easier or because it was such a beautiful time of day for visitors to get their first look at these lovely islands.

As they approached, Bali did not appear very different from Tahiti—a lush tropical island rising to jagged mountain peaks out of the blue water. The multicolored coral was not as brightly noticeable around Bali as it had been around Tahiti.

In spite of a day's layover in Sydney, it had been a longer trip than Wendy had expected. Familiar as she was with the map of the area that hung on her office wall, she hadn't fully visualized the vast distances of the Pacific and the International Date Line. The confusion of time and distance vanished as she stepped from the plane into the soft tropical morning and heard the familiar cry of the myna bird greeting the day.

Customs clearance was smooth and orderly with a touch of Oriental courtesy. A microbus waited at the exit to take guests to the Sanur beach hotels. All roads in Bali lead to Denpasar, the capital, so the bus turned in that direction. As they passed rice fields and pagoda-shaped temples, it was apparent that Bali is a part of the Orient, geographically and culturally.

In Denpasar Wendy tried to concentrate on the interesting contrasts of architecture—Balinese, Dutch colonial, and modern. But an even more fascinating pageant was passing in the streets with buses, taxis, horse-drawn carts, motorcycles, bicycles, and even bicycle-powered rickshaws all traveling on the left side of the road.

"Pemetjutan Palace," the driver announced, pointing to a series of shaded pavilions. Wendy caught a glimpse of beautiful wood carvings decorating pillars and doorways.

As the bus turned toward Sanur, it passed an open market where women in colorful costumes and turbans offered a wide variety of goods, both common and exotic. Flat reed baskets were piled high with strange fruit and foods. Colorful materials hung above the heads of seated vendors. A blend of unidentifiable spices drifted through the open window of the bus. The market offered the promise of an intriguing morning of browsing and shopping.

At Sanur beach the microbus passed the gleaming ten-story Bali Beach Hotel, a bit of transplanted America. A few miles farther down the beach, the bus turned in to the lovely garden of Tandjung Sari with its individual thatched bungalows and exotic tropical plants nestled among palm trees. As Wendy signed the guest register, she noticed that a group arranged by Personal World Tours was staying there.

Wendy's cottage was a modified A-frame with a thatched roof and large windows. A ceiling fan turned lazily above beautiful teakwood furniture. The floor was mat-covered, and there were rattan chairs on the lanai. Like the island itself, the room was a charming blend of South Seas and Oriental influences.

Wendy changed into shorts and a sleeveless, knotted midriff shirt and went out to explore her new surroundings. Neatly marked paths meandered among ponds, streams, and waterfalls. She stopped to watch giant goldfish swimming in the pools. Brilliant tropical birds hopped along the path and flashed from tree to tree—baby-pink cockatoos and bright, turquoise blue birds. They were so unafraid of humans that one of the cockatoos hopped up on her basket-purse and began pulling out a tissue.

One path led down to the beach. The sand had very little coral and was soft beneath Wendy's feet. Farther out the coral created a white breakwater where the deep blue of the ocean met the pale blue water of the lagoon. As Wendy watched the water, two Balinese boys approached, selling postcards and fine wood carvings of dancers, temples, and animals. Wendy bought several cards showing colorful Balinese dancers, but decided to buy her mother a carving from a store that would pack and ship it.

Back at her cabin Wendy had just settled down to the task of writing postcards when there was a knock on her door. "Miss Devin?"

"Yes."

"I am Muda Tamjong. I am the Balinese guide for Personal World Tours. The clerk told me you were staying here. I want to welcome you to Bali and offer you my services if there is anything I can do to help you." He handed her his card.

"Thank you," Wendy answered the handsome young man. "I haven't made any plans yet, but if I need anything I'll call you."

"I am taking one of your tours to a Barong play and Kris dances tonight, and I would be happy to have you join us."

"That sounds very interesting. I have heard a good deal about Balinese dancers."

"We'll meet in the lounge at eight."

Wendy went back to her postcards. She sent one to her mother, filled with as much detail of beautiful Bali as she could cram in. She would postpone writing to Mr. Vance, her boss, until after the dances when she would have a firsthand report on one of their tours in Bali.

That left Marvin. Wendy couldn't remember ever delaying so long acknowledging a gift. She addressed one of the cards and then paused, chewing thoughtfully on the end of her pen. Once she had said, "Thank you for the lovely charm," there seemed to be nothing more to say. Even "Having a wonderful time," or "Wish you were here," seemed inappropriate to the groom who had failed to show up for their wedding. She searched through her thoughts for something she might say about Bali. The rice fields—she had passed workers planting rice and hadn't even thought of Marvin. It had once seemed so important, helping him in his work to find a superior rice hybrid. Was she letting wounded pride stand in the way of her dedication to making a worthwhile commitment? She thought of the contrast between the serious scientist in San Francisco and charming, carefree Erick and remembered her disappointment that Erick hadn't asked about seeing her in Bangkok. It was hardly a city where two people could expect to meet by chance, and calling all the hotels would be quite a project. Then too, there was the mysterious girl in Bangkok whom Migin had mentioned.

With an effort, Wendy returned her attention to the postcard to Marvin, managing to fill it with general comments from her casual observations.

As Wendy entered the lounge a few minutes before eight, Muda came forward to greet her. "We are so glad you could join us."

Wendy was grateful that he did not make a special point of introducing her to the group. She wanted their reactions to the tour to be as natural as possible. A plump middle-aged lady came puffing into the lounge. Muda nodded to her, took a quick head count, and announced, "Our bus is here. Shall we go?"

A microbus similar to the one which had brought her from the airport took them along the coast to a large white building on the grounds of the temple. They entered the dance pavilion through intricately carved doors depicting a jungle world of animals, giving favored position to the monkeys.

Their group was seated on brocaded cushions as girls in colorful embroidered silk sarongs served them Chinese tea and delicious cakes made of raw sugar and nuts. Balinese women must be among the most beautiful in the world, Wendy thought, with their flawless ginger-colored complexions, large almond eyes, and jet-black hair coiled on top of shapely heads. Even the serving girls moved with the grace of trained dancers.

The *gamelan*, an orchestra composed of gongs of many sizes and shapes, as well as flutes, drums, cymbals, and bamboo clicking instruments, began its vibrant beat. Through the split temple gate that formed a backdrop for the play appeared the Barong, the mystical creature with a long swayback and curved tail, which represents the forces of good. The two men inside the fantastic costume sidestepped and whirled, snapped at the *gamelan* and swished flies with its tail. The Barong was joined by a dancer in monkey costume and three men wearing masks who danced a comedy number as prelude to the play.

The play was an involved, ritualistic story of the struggle between the good Barong and the bad Rangda, who practices black magic and takes many forms, both animal and human.

During intermission two beautiful Legong dancers became divine nymphs wrapped in gold brocade and wearing crowns of gold and flowers. Their dance combined graceful, dynamic gestures and subtle movements of eyes and fingers.

The play concluded with a frenzied battle between the disciples of evil and the Kris dancers, the army of the good Barong, holding carved and jeweled ritual swords of great beauty. The fight had no victors to show that the war against evil is eternal. At the conclusion of the performance, the temple priest sprinkled the Kris dancers with holy water and then killed a chicken, spilling its blood on the ground to ward off evil spirits. The gesture made Wendy shudder.

In spite of the rather gruesome ending, the play and dancing made for a delightful evening. A young architect from Los Angeles had been particularly attentive to Wendy in the noncommitted manner of travelers who expect to go their separate ways when the encounter ends. Had that also been true of her romance with Erick? Wendy wondered.

Wendy had been so favorably impressed with Muda and the tour that her intended postcard to Mr. Vance became a letter. Muda had been charming and knowledgeable, speaking excellent English, and remaining particularly tactful when the plump matron showed signs of becoming ill at the sight of the chicken blood.

Wendy was already awake the next morning when the myna birds began their dawn symphony. She slipped quickly into her bikini and matching smock cover and ran down to the shore to await the glorious burst of the tropical sunrise. As the flaming rim spread molten bronze over the Indian Ocean, a cockatoo began to scold raucously. Looking up the beach, Wendy saw a tall blond American come striding toward her. He moved with a swift boyish gait just like Erick's—it was Erick!

Wendy ran to meet him. He swept her off her feet in a dizzying whirl and smothered her with a lingering kiss.

"You fly very well," he told her, recalling her words at their first meeting as he set her back on her feet.

"You must have done some flying yourself to be here," she countered, breaking off in midsentence as she remembered the other girls who had run to greet his arrival—first Migin, then Niki. What was there about this dashing adventurer that caused girls to fly into his arms? "With you, things are always so sudden," Niki had said. Was it just the delight of his sudden appearance? Wendy wondered. "How was the dive?" she asked in a more restrained tone.

"Marvelous. Migin thinks they found a new species. Her father will have it checked by the Cousteau researchers. If it is, he wants to name it "Mignette," but she wants to call it "Haape.""

"I like that, a 'Haape fish.' What's it like?"

"It's a small fish, electric-blue with bronze overtones—rather like that sunrise," he said.

"That was beautiful, wasn't it?" she agreed as they settled on the sand, enjoying the morning newness of the beach marked only by their own footprints.

"I thought you would be on your way to Bangkok," Wendy said.

"I am. Bali is on the way. Just stopped off to see an old friend."

Wendy eyed him suspiciously. "Does he own a resort?"

"No, just a boat—or several of them: a cruiser for diving and the local version of the outrigger."

"Your friends seem to have a monopoly on boating and diving in the Far East."

Erick laughed. "I guess our group in Bangkok was a little boat happy. Both Tom and Mike have built their business around them. You'll have to meet Mike."

"Is he married?"

"No. On second thought, maybe you shouldn't meet him. He's a real charmer."

"That seems to be a characteristic of the group too," Wendy teased.

"I hope you don't have plans for the day," Erick said with a sudden hesitation.

"No, just enjoying things as they come in the South Seas spirit."

"Good. Do you mind riding a motorcycle?"

"No, though I have never tried it," she replied honestly, remembering her mother's dictum against motorcycles at home.

"It's the best way to get where we're going. I have one rented for the day."

"Pretty sure of yourself, weren't you?" she bantered.

"He pulled her to her feet and settled the matter with a quick kiss. "Go change, and I'll meet you in front of the office."

A few minutes later Erick helped Wendy onto a saddlelike seat fastened to the frame of the bike, and instructed her to put her feet on the pegs protruding from the rear wheel. "Just put your arms around my waist and hang on," he told her.

Wendy took a secure hold of Erick and braced herself for the roaring start she had observed of cyclists at home. But Erick started the sputtering machine smoothly and they breezed along at a moderate speed to enjoy the passing scenery.

At Denpasar they slowed to enjoy the beauty of Pura Djagatnata, the temple newly built of white coral. The split gate framed its graceful carved tower gleaming in the morning sun.

At the main intersection, Erick waved a greeting to its demon guardian. "So no evil will come to the spot," he explained.

In the swirl of converging traffic, Wendy hoped he was right about claiming there were rarely any accidents. At the corner of the market they turned north through a residential area where chickens, children, and housewives mingled in the confusion of the morning's activities.

As they reached the outskirts of the city, most of the traffic consisted of bicycles carrying an amazing assortment of items, some of them very large and unwieldy. They passed one man with a live pig stretched out on a rack on the back of his bike.

"He's passed out from distillery mash," Erick explained. "The farmer has to deliver him before he comes to."

The road climbed steadily and the size and age of the trees increased. Erick stopped before a temple gate in a heavily forested area. "Bukit Sari, the Monkey Forest. It was established by one of the rajas as a refuge for the monkeys. The forest is considered sacred and no one is allowed to chop wood here. Legend says that these monkeys were part of the army of the monkey general Hanuman who killed the giant Rawana in the Ramayana epic Hindu poem."

"You know so much about the customs and religions of Asia," said Wendy. "Are you interested in religions?"

"I'm interested in people, and their customs and beliefs are a part of them. But we're getting very serious about a fun place. Come on, you'll see."

At the gate they bought bags of peanuts. The attendant placed the small paper envelopes of nuts in a larger plastic bag with a handle. "That's to keep the monkeys from snatching the peanuts away from you and running off with them," Erick explained.

Small, sprite monkeys seemed to be everywhere. As they walked along the path to the temple, both Wendy and Erick handed out peanuts to the monkeys gathered around them. "Hey, stop that," Erick scolded a particularly large monkey, who was walking along behind them collecting the nuts from the smaller monkeys. "He's king of this region, and it looks like he's a real dictator."

Erick picked up a small monkey who had been forced to surrender his nut, and set him on his shoulder. The monkey ran his fingers through Erick's hair, examined his ear, and gobbled down the peanuts Erick handed him. Safe beyond the reach of the king, he was lord of all he surveyed.

Another small victim of the king's greed studied the situation a moment and jumped up onto Wendy's shoulder. He ate a peanut sitting on her shoulder and then ran around her neck to the other shoulder. The empty shoulder was filled immediately by another monkey. A third one decided that her purse looked like a good refuge from the big monkey.

Eventually they came to a moss-covered temple, it too filled with monkeys. A beautiful raised teakwood platform stood in the temple area. "Is it for dances?" Wendy asked.

"Yes, once a year a festival is held here to honor the gods who look after the forest and the forest creatures, particularly the monkeys." Erick answered.

Their walk back to the main gate became a regular parade with at least thirty monkeys following Wendy and Erick. Occasionally a bolder one would run in front of them, hold out his hand and with a "chi-chi-chi" demand more peanuts. They took shells or anything else that was offered.

"That one reminds me of a major I know," said Erick of a large monkey commanding the smaller ones to make way for him.

"I think I see some familiar faces here too," Wendy added as they waved good-bye to the monkeys. One bright monkey copied their waving motion.

Laughing, Erick helped Wendy back on the motorcycle. "Wendy Devin, you are my kind of girl," he said, brushing her cheek lightly with a kiss.

But are you my kind of man? Wendy wondered as she clasped her arms around his waist. Could I spend my life frolicking with this Peter Pan, this boy who never grew up?

"I think we better call it a day," Erick said when they got back to Wendy's bungalow. "I hope the motorcycle won't make you stiff."

"I feel fine. It's been fun," Wendy answered.

"Try to sleep in. Tomorrow is the night of the full moon, and you won't want to miss it."

"Sounds spooky, like Halloween."

"It is. How about my picking you up around noon for a sail in one of Mike's outriggers? That should leave us fresh for the evening."

"Providing I get to meet the charming Mike," she teased.

"Ah, the price of friendship," Erick mourned as he mounted the motorcycle and took off in one smooth motion.

When Wendy's feathered alarm, the myna, sounded the next morning, she realized she really was tired from the previous day's motorcycling. It was sheer luxury to turn over and go back to sleep. She was just finishing a late-morning brunch of tropical fruit with crisp rolls and cheese, a legacy of Bali's former Dutch occupants, when Erick arrived. They walked the short distance to the dock.

"Where did you find that Colleen out here?" a big red-haired Irishman asked in a brogue deliberately thickened, as he stared approvingly into Wendy's green eyes.

"Wendy Devin, this is Mike O'Connor, and you've been warned about his blarney."

"Now, would you look who's talkin'," Mike responded. Turning to Wendy, he said, "I know the night of the full moon is supposed to bring out the good spirits, but I didn't expect leprechauns and an Irish lass to celebrate it with. You are going to Turtle Island with me tonight, aren't you?"

"We'll go wherever you say, as long as Wendy gets to see one of the temple festivals of the full moon," Erick answered.

"I'd like to sail in my prao across the harbor to Serangan, the sea temple. It's one of the few dedicated to Dewi Danu, goddess of the waters. The Balinese are not seafaring people. They believe demons and ghosts hide in the ocean. Very few of them can even swim. The Polynesians brought the praos to Bali, and there should be a lot of them there tonight," said Mike.

"I'm anxious to try one," said Erick.

"There isn't a finer outrigger in all the South Seas. That triangular sail, shot like an arrowhead into the bow of the boat, gives it the speed and grace of a bird. If you're ready, we can get started."

Under Mike's expert guidance, the prao skimmed the still waters of Badung Strait. "It seems as if we are flying or gliding over the water," said Wendy. Mike beamed with delight at his guest as the breeze swept her tumble of light-brown hair back from her pixie face, making her green eyes sparkle.

"What in the world is that?" Wendy asked, pointing to a brilliantly colored fishlike form in the sky.

"That is a giant kite. Some of them are as much as twenty-five feet long," answered Mike.

"How do people get them up in the air?"

"You'll see when we get closer to the island."

The next kite they spotted looked like a sea gull, another like a box in rainbow hues. "There's one of our friends," said Erick, pointing to a giant replica of a monkey. This time they were close enough so that Wendy could see that the kite was being towed by a prao.

"That's how they get enough speed to launch them," Mike explained.

"Are they just for the celebration tonight?" Wendy asked.

"No. Children like to fly the giant kites anytime. In fact, they are so popular the government has asked people to shorten the strings so they won't distract pilots on their descent for the airport across the harbor."

Though they were early, Mike had as much trouble finding a place to anchor the prao as a motorist trying to park for a parade. Finally, two smiling Balinese eased their boats over and made room for him to nose the slender craft onto the sandy beach.

The trio walked up the beach to the turtle pens, from which Turtle Island received its nickname. "I never dreamed a turtle could get so big," said Wendy watching a giant sea turtle paddle lazily through the shallow water of the pen. "Why are they penned up?"

"They are being fattened on sea grass for special banquets. Sea turtle is considered a great delicacy."

Excited shouting came from a circle of men partly

hidden in a grove of palm trees. Wendy started in the direction of the noise. "That's a cock fight," said Erick. "They get a little bloody—I don't think you would care for it."

Wrinkling her nose in distaste, Wendy turned in the opposite direction and followed a winding path leading to gaily decorated stands. There were cakes of ground nuts and raw sugar like those Wendy had sampled the first evening. Children eagerly bought coconut candies and other bright-colored sweets. The shy, smiling children stole furtive glances at the big red-haired man and the equally tall blond one towering over the crowd, but they did not seem to be frightened by them.

The *gamelan* orchestra had begun to play by the time they arrived at the temple. There were a number of solo dances as the crowd gathered; then the play began. Like the one Wendy had seen earlier, it was a dance-drama based on the Hindu epic, the *Ramayana*, depicting the battle between good and evil in many guises. Here, however, the audience became a part of the play as the familiar story unfolded. Children in the front scampered back when the demons came too close. The audience hissed at the villain and applauded the hero as for a melodrama, but with more serious support for good over evil.

The moon shone high in the sky when Mike eased the prao away from Turtle Island. Wendy leaned her head on Erick's shoulder, convinced that the Balinese were right in believing there is magic on the night of the full moon.

The sand and sea were patterned with shimmering white and even the ancient wood of the dock gleamed with a silvery sheen when Wendy and Erick bade Mike good-bye with repeated thanks for a delightful evening. Still carrying their shoes, which they had removed in the boat, they walked hand-in-hand along the edge of the water where the moonstruck current made eddying pools of light around their ankles. No one intruded on their ethereal domain.

"Did you say you learned about canoes at summer camp?" Erick asked.

"Yes," she answered, puzzled and a little annoyed by his unusual question.

"Then I'll bet you have your bikini on under your slacks and shirt."

Wendy nodded, flushed with embarrassment, and wished the night was not so light that he could see her rising color.

"Good! I'll beat you into the water," he called, rapidly shedding shirt and trousers to reveal that he too had worn a swimsuit.

Caught by surprise, she was still struggling with a balky shirt button when he raced into the surf and dived into a cresting wave in a graceful arc. Sprinting through the gently curling surf behind him, she stopped to watch as his powerful strokes carried him smoothly through the water while shimmering spray reflecting the moonlight outlined his athletic body in luminescence.

Erick circled back in her direction and she swam to meet him. The indigo water was warm and silky, more conducive to languid play than a vigorous swim. Like dolphins they dived and splashed, tumbled and frolicked. She lost sight of him beyond a rolling wave and stopped to tread water and look about her in confusion. Suddenly he emerged beside her, the brilliant moonlight gleaming off the wetness of his blond hair, handsome face, and broad shoulders. He was a Viking prince rising from the sea. Laughing, he caught her in the circle of one powerful arm while easy strokes with his other arm kept them both afloat. Without effort he carried her along with him until his feet touched bottom, then his other arm came around her. The ebbing tide brought her floating form against the shiny, wet muscles of his broad chest. His hands slid sensuously down her water-slick body; then suddenly he let her go. Instinctively, she flung her arms around his neck for support. Laughing, he closed his arms around her and kissed her, at first casually as they had before, then persuasively leading her passion to respond to his.

Her whole being seemed suspended in the warm, caressing water, the tropic air, the moonlight. There was a threat of breathless madness in the lustrous radiance of the full moon. She wasn't sure she could retreat from that madness if he did not.

With a deeper, huskier, more emotion-filled laugh, he caught her in his arms and lifted her from the water as though she were a child. He carried her to the beach and stood her unsteadily on her feet. Throwing back his head, he gave a long, low howl like a wolf baying at the moon. Wendy laughed in spite of herself and the enchantment was broken. The moon slid discreetly behind a cloud.

"Playtime is over," Erick said as they walked back to her cottage. "I have to report for duty tomorrow, so I'll be leaving on the early-morning plane."

"Can I see you off?" she asked.

"Airports are for takeoff and landing, not for greetings or good-byes," he said firmly. He held her close and kissed her tenderly, then turned and walked resolutely away without looking back.

CHAPTER FIVE

Have I left the magic behind, Wendy wondered. She looked out the airplane window at the rice paddies of Thailand stretching smooth and green as the turf of a football field, with the *klongs*—canals of brown water—looking like yardage markers. In a few minutes her plane landed in Bangkok in the shimmering brightness of midday, far different from her misty morning arrivals in Tahiti and Bali.

He didn't ask where I would be in Bangkok, Wendy mused as she collected her overnight case and the flight bag of travel information. Maybe that was the way it had been with Niki, when Erick went back to the mysterious girl in Bangkok.

The terminal building was simple and functional without distinctive features. "Miss Wendy?" asked a teen-age Thai boy as she emerged from customs.

"Yes," she answered, trying to gather a clue as to

the boy's identity from the bright red baseball cap he wore at a rakish angle.

"I'm Tahn," he said, wiping his hand on his short pants before extending it in greeting. "Captain Erick said I should be your guide in Bangkok."

"How did you know who I was?" she asked as Tahn pumped her hand enthusiastically.

"He showed me a picture—very pretty with flowers on your head."

The one taken at Club Mediterranée, Wendy thought, remembering the enchanted moments before Niki had appeared.

Tahn picked up her suitcase and led her out of the terminal to the line of waiting taxis. Tahn and the driver engaged in a lively dialogue in Thai. Wendy caught frequent mention of *baht*, the money of Thailand. Finally an agreement was reached and Tahn helped Wendy into the cab, put her suitcase in the trunk, and climbed in beside her.

"How did Erick know when I would arrive?" Wendy asked as the taxi turned into the main highway from Don Muang Airport.

"There is just one plane a day from Bali, so I come yesterday and today. If you do not come today, tomorrow."

"I'm sorry you came and waited yesterday," Wendy told him.

"Waiting very good," Tahn replied. "Three men like my red cap and motion for me to be their guide to the taxi. I carry their suitcases. I tell them about Thailand and our customs. I tell them that in Thailand you must bargain with the taxi driver for the price to go to

Bangkok. When we go out to the taxi the man bargains with the driver. He does not bargain very good, but when the price is less than the driver say first, he is very pleased. He give me a big tip. Now I can hire boat for me to water-ski."

"Do you like to ski?"

"Yes. Captain Erick teach me when I am a small boy before he go back to America."

"Where do you ski?"

"Pattaya. My village is near Pattaya."

"If I go to Pattaya, will you teach me to ski?" Wendy asked, hoping to avoid the awkward moments when Erick had to teach her to snorkel or ride a motorcycle.

"I would teach you good," Tahn answered. "Erick teach me good."

"He is a good teacher," Wendy said knowingly.

They had reached the noisy, bustling outskirts of Bangkok where small shops heaped to the ceiling with their wares competed for space with shabby apartment buildings.

"Where did you tell the driver to take us?" Wendy asked as the taxi turned from the crowded highway onto a broad avenue lined with handsome, modern buildings.

"The Siam Hotel. Captain Erick said you would like the garden. It has monkeys."

The taxi skirted a clear, lotus-filled reflecting pool and stopped before a replica of an old Siamese palace. The sharply peaked red roof swept heavenward at the tips of the eaves. Carved monkeys, guardians against evil spirits, adorned the ridge pole and the corners.

The magic of fairy tales might well be lurking here, Wendy decided.

"I must go back to Pattaya," Tahn told her as he deposited her suitcase beside the desk. "Tomorrow I ski."

"Do I bargain with my guide for his fee too?" Wendy asked lightly, seeking some clue as to what was expected.

"One does not accept pay from friends. You are my friend because you are a friend of Erick," Tahn replied, suddenly very serious. He placed his fingertips together, prayerlike, and bowed deeply in a gesture called a *wai*, then turned and walked away.

Wendy was concerned that she had offended her new friend, but as he reached the door he doffed his red cap and waved it in a wide sweeping arc, then bounded down the steps with schoolboy abandon.

A friend of Erick, that seemed to be the magic word, Wendy thought—Tom and Migin in Mooréa, Mike in Bali, and Tahn waiting to meet her when she arrived in Bangkok.

Wendy's room was very modern with touches of Thailand in its decor—a woven cotton bedspread and drapes dyed in the subtle blends of Thai silk, a low teak table surrounded by cushions. She spent the afternoon relaxing in its air-conditioned comfort while the realities of time and place caught up with her.

The heat of the day was giving way to an evening breeze from distant mountains when Wendy crossed the *klong* which divided the broad lawn from the garden. It was a cool, inviting haven under a canopy of tropical trees. A small stream gurgled under arching oriental bridges into lotus-filled pools. A pair of honey-colored monkeys frolicked across her path and sat scolding her from an orchid-draped tree. Brilliant birds of many exotic species turned in their cages to watch a dispute among a group of small monkeys. A large black monkey with a white ruff around his neck grunted commands which seemed to settle the matter.

"I see you've met The General," said Erick close behind her.

Wendy turned in surprise and had to restrain the urge to rush toward him. Erick showed no hesitation as he bridged the distance between them in two long strides, took her in his arms, and kissed her tenderly. "Welcome to Bangkok," he said, releasing her reluctantly.

"It has been a nice welcome, starting with Tahn to greet me and now you," Wendy answered.

"He's quite a boy," said Erick fondly. "He was such a shy, skinny kid when he first began to hang around the docks in Pattaya."

"He says you taught him to ski."

"Yes, he was my lookout boy."

"Lookout boy?"

"When a lone skier rents a Thai motorboat, he has to take a boy along to watch out for swimmers and other boats while he skis. 'Look out' was the first English Tahn learned. We'll have to try some skiing this weekend."

They crossed one of the gracefully arching bridges leading to the street, and strolled along a broad boulevard crowded with people enjoying the early twilight hours.

"Does that little shrine mark something special?" Wendy asked, noting people bringing flowers and candles to a white-and-gold shrine the size of a large birdhouse on a pedestal.

"That's a spirit house for the guardian spirit which controls good and bad fortune on the property. That one is in front of the visitor's bureau. People who make a living from the tourist business bring offerings."

The smell of tropical flowers and the shouts of children at play filled the deepening twilight as they crossed the edge of Lumpini Park. "I want you to see the city spread out at your feet," said Erick when they had dodged through the busy traffic circle to the tall imposing Dusit Thani Hotel.

They climbed the steps to the main entrance where a small crowd was gathered. Suddenly the automatic door swung open and a colorfully dressed attendant appeared, pulling and prodding a baby elephant. Several bellboys shoved and urged him along from behind.

"'Is that the way they treat their guests?" Wendy quipped.

"Only that one," Erick answered. "He's the hotel's mascot, and sometimes on a hot afternoon he feels the cool air inside when the doors open, steps on the automatic door pad, and goes in. I don't know what would cause him to go in this time of day—perhaps a child with some peanuts. Even though he is just a baby, it's quite a job to get him out. An older elephant would be trained, but that one is popular because he's small."

An express elevator carried them quickly to the glass-enclosed tower lounge. "It's breathtaking," said Wendy, looking out at the skyline pierced at intervals by the graceful spires of temples and palaces. The Chao Phya River bounding the city was a busy thoroughfare of boats which looked like toys from their high vantage point.

"I wish I could show you the city tomorrow," said Erick, "but the squadron is shorthanded and I have to fly an Air-Evac to Chiengmai. It will be three-day duty."

"An Air-Evac?" Wendy asked.

"Our helicopter squadron is assigned to the hospital here and we're sort of an airborne ambulance when anyone at an outlying base needs to come in to Bangkok for special medical care."

It was hard for Wendy to imagine Erick, her modern Viking, flying a slow, awkward helicopter. A sleek, swept-wing supersonic jet would have seemed more his style, she thought as she watched the lights of a modern airliner illuminate the ancient spires. Reluctantly she turned from the observation window, where all of picturesque Bangkok lay spread at her feet—just as he had promised.

Back on street level Erick waved away the doorman and the waiting taxis and paused to give the independent little elephant a pat. Casually he hailed an odd-looking, three-wheeled vehicle with open sides and a canvas top. The driver pulled to the curb and they climbed up on the small carriage seat. "A *samlor*," explained Erick. "Out in the country they are pedicabs powered by a bicycle, but for safety in Bangkok traffic they have to be motorized."

"Around the park," he instructed as the driver deftly maneuvered the small vehicle into traffic. It was a soft and starlit night filled with the musical sounds of the Thai language and the laughter of children. Couples paddled small boats on the lake while others spread picnics beneath the palm trees. Wendy nestled contentedly against Erick's shoulder. It was the perfect carriage to take the princess back to her palace, even if the palace was only a replica.

Apparently playtime is not over, Wendy mused as she leaned against her door and brushed the back of her hand across her lips, still tingling from Erick's goodnight kiss. Had the mystery girl in Bangkok Migin had mentioned stopped waiting for Erick's return? Even if she had not, Wendy wondered if she really wanted to continue this playtime romance. As a travel agent, she knew that summer romance was part of a working girl's dream vacation. Though hers was a business trip, Erick had certainly made it a dream come true. But where would it end? Was she building up to another letdown? If she let herself love Erick in the way she knew she could, the hurt could go far deeper than the burst of Irish temper and humiliation she had known with Marvin. At least with Erick away for the next three days she would have time to think things out. . . .

The next morning Wendy was awakened by sounds of traffic and people going about their business, and recalled the peaceful calm of the Pacific islands. But there was one place she particularly wanted to see. She dressed quickly, and the doorman finally got her a taxi, in spite of the rush of early-morning traffic.

Wendy walked through the gates of the Grand Palace and paused before the real-life setting of her favorite musical, "The King and I." She stood in a wonderland created by succeeding rulers of Siam who had each sought to outdo his predecessors in splendor. A pink-pillared palace in the center was flanked by gleaming white ones on either side, while a carved and gilded gazebo united them in an architectural whole. She mounted the steps of the gleaming central building, half-expecting to find the legendary King of Siam holding court inside. The intricate carving, rich silks, brocades, and gold leaf of the ceremonial room in which she found herself made her feel as if Anna and the King might have just left. The nine-tiered white canopy, like a giant wedding cake above the royal throne, reminded her that this palace was still used for state functions by Thailand's present royalty. Her guide led her from one dazzling room to another, and finally through a gate to the most beautiful building in Siam, the Temple of the Emerald Buddha. The five-hundred-year-old image inside was carved from a single piece of jade. The exquisitely rendered figure appeared quite small atop the high, elaborate gold altar designed to represent an aerial chariot.

Though it was a busy weekday morning, an unending succession of Thais came to pay their respects. Here the past and the present flowed smoothly together.

Before returning to her hotel, Wendy stopped at the office of her company's tour representative to see if any mail had preceded her to Bangkok. There were two letters: one bore the distinctive seal of Personal World Tours, the other Marvin's hasty scrawl. Wendy turned Marvin's letter over in her hand with a troubled feeling, then put both letters in her purse to read at leisure when she got back to her room.

She walked down the street, pausing before a window of beautifully draped and displayed Thai silk. The colors were soft and subtly blended. Though she wanted to send some to her mother, Wendy was experienced enough at travel shopping to wait until she became more familiar with values and prices. The next window displayed blue star sapphires winking invitingly in beautifully crafted rings and pendants. This was an indulgence Wendy had promised herself, but again the words were wait and compare. At the corner she hailed a taxi. Settling back to watch the colorful passing panorama, she realized how tired she was.

Once propped up on her bed in the air-conditioned comfort of her room, Wendy turned her attention to her mail. The letter from Mr. Vance was short, wishing her a good trip. Apparently their letters had crossed in the mail.

Wendy was surprised by the length of Marvin's letter—several neatly folded pages of lined note paper—because he was usually so preoccupied. She started to read with as little enthusiasm as she would have had for an overdue bill:

"Dear Wendy, I hope by now you realize how important it was that I should confer with Dr. Pridi when he was here—even though it was (or should have been) our wedding day—and have forgiven me."

She paused, trying to sort out her tangled feelings about Marvin. She did not feel anger; that had passed in the first flash of her Irish temper. Wounded pride? Perhaps, but mostly confusion about the place of Marvin's work in their relationship, and its importance to him—to her. What role, if any, did Erick play in her jumbled emotions? Finding no answers, Wendy continued Marvin's letter:

"The analysis of the rice cultures has exceeded our expectations."

Wendy felt again the old glow of pride in Marvin's dedication to the needs of hungry people.

"I walked down to the marina yesterday evening to watch the sailboats coming in—the way we did so often. The fog was beginning to roll through the Golden Gate so that the bridge seemed to be floating on the clouds."

Wendy could almost feel the tingling coolness of the fog on her face. Marvin seemed to have anticipated her feelings far from home, leading her memory on a wave of nostalgia. The same cautious voice that had warned her of being swept off her feet by the dashing, romantic Erick, now warned that Marvin seemed to be devoting the full resources of his brilliant mind to regaining her love and loyalty. It was a thought both flattering and frightening.

CHAPTER SIX

"Miss Wendy!" shouted Tahn as she stepped from the bus in Pattaya Saturday morning.

"How did you know this time when I would be coming?" Wendy asked.

"I do not know. Every Saturday I come to the morning bus. If someone ask where is boat harbor, I show them. Sometimes I get to be lookout boy."

"Do you get to ski when you are lookout?"

"No, only Mr. Erick let me ski when he rents boat; and Miss Jane."

"Miss Jane?"

"She is friend of Mr. Erick long time ago."

"Is she still here?"

"No, she lives in Bangkok at the hospital."

Feeling as if she had been prying without intending to, Wendy did not pursue the subject further.

"You want I take your suitcase in the hotel?" asked

Tahn, indicating the sprawling lodge before which the bus had stopped.

"Please do," Wendy answered. She didn't need help with the small overnight case, but she could see it pleased Tahn to help. They crossed the beautifully landscaped garden, skirted the crowded pool, and entered the lodge, which was open across the front to the cool morning breeze off the Gulf of Siam.

The bellboy seemed confused when Tahn clung tenaciously to Wendy's suitcase, but bowed politely and showed her to her room.

"You go ski and I be your lookout?" Tahn asked hopefully.

"No, I want to learn to ski, and you be my teacher so I won't be so dumb when Erick comes this afternoon."

"Mr. Erick is coming today?" Tahn asked eagerly.

Wendy nodded. "Go wait for me by the pool until I get my suit on, and we'll get started with that lesson."

"Do we rent a boat here?" Wendy asked as she joined Tahn.

"No, we go see my boat man at the harbor."

"Let's take a *samlor*," Wendy suggested. She was surprised when Tahn climbed into the little pedicab without preliminary bargaining. "Don't you bargain with the *samlor* driver?" she asked.

"No, only with taxi driver. *Samlor* driver charge everyone five baht to boat harbor."

Wendy arranged to rent a motorboat and skis for an hour. "You go first, and I'll watch you," she told the delighted Tahn. She took the seat in the rear of the boat while Tahn sat on the edge of the dock and put on the skis. The driver tossed him the tow rope and accelerated rapidly away from the dock so that Tahn took off in a jet of motion. When the boat reached deep water, the driver cut into a series of sharp turns, leaving Tahn to jump the wake of the boat as they crossed and recrossed it. On a straight run down the harbor Tahn did a series of tricks, some on only one ski. It was a showy performance reminding Wendy of a small boy hanging by his knees in a tree to impress the new girl on the block.

"You try it?" Tahn asked Wendy.

"Might as well," she replied, hoping her experience skiing in the snow of the Sierras would be of some help. The skis did not feel too awkward on her feet. Though Tahn had used only one hand, Wendy grasped the tow rope firmly in both hands. Feeling the rope begin to take up, Wendy flexed her knees as she had done on the snow. The skis leveled and for a brief moment she was up on the water. But she was too far up and over she went.

"You all right?" Tahn asked with concern as Wendy emerged sputtering and gasping.

"No worse than when I make a bad dive, just swallowed a lot of water."

Tahn burst out with the laugh he had been surpressing. "Want to try it again?"

"Only way to learn," she answered, collecting the skis as they floated nearby.

"Hold back till the boat pull you up," Tahn directed.

Following his instructions, Wendy was able to glide

smoothly off the dock and balance herself above the skis, but she was unable to rise from a sitting position as she dragged the bottom of her bikini through the water. She followed behind the boat several hundred yards, struggling to get up on her feet, but finally had to drop the rope. Water-skiing was definitely not a skill to learn in one easy lesson.

"That's enough. You can finish out the hour," said Wendy after three more attempts, each only slightly more successful than the last.

"Can I take my brothers?" Tahn asked.

"Sure," Wendy answered, and Tahn made a great sweeping wave to two smaller boys on the dock. As Wendy climbed out onto the dock, the smaller of the two scrambled into the boat while the older one hurriedly donned the skis. He was a small copy of Tahn. As the boat sped down the harbor, he tried valiantly to duplicate Tahn's earlier performance.

Wendy took a *samlor* back to the lodge for some sunning—the reason she had given Erick for coming down to the beach in the morning rather than waiting until he got off work.

"Done just the way I like it," said Erick's familiar voice as he pressed a finger on Wendy's shoulder as if testing a cake.

"I must have dozed off. Feels like you found me just in time," she answered, a warm inner glow matching the warmth of her sun-drenched shoulders.

"I think you need a swim—last one in is a lobster," called Erick, racing for the gently breaking surf.

The water was cool and refreshing as the two of them splashed and bobbed in the surf, which broke too sharply for serious swimming. Fun and a zest for living seemed to be part of everything Erick did.

As they ran back up the beach, Wendy was surprised to meet a boy leading a small elephant.

"I'll bet you haven't ridden an elephant," said Erick.

"Nooo," answered Wendy dubiously.

"That one looks about your size," he said indicating the approaching animal, whose head was not much higher than Wendy's. After negotiating with the elephant boy, Erick held his hands together to help Wendy mount. The elephant's hair was extremely coarse as it rubbed against her wet skin. The boy led the elephant by its trunk in slow, lumbering stomps around the swimming pool. He cut around one of the corners so close that Wendy thought they might fall in. Erick took her camera from her beach bag and they posed for pictures. The boy handed Wendy peanuts so that the elephant would reach his trunk up to her in a trumpeting pose. When Erick finished taking pictures, the elephant knelt on its front knees to let her know the ride was over. As he started down, Wendy thought she might pitch off over his head, but his motion was slow and deliberate and she was able to balance herself and slide off easily.

"The elephant follows the boy around just like a big dog," said Wendy as she and Erick continued down the beach.

"That just about describes it. Much of the heavy work in northern Thailand is done by elephants— particularly in the teak forests. If a family can give their son a baby elephant when he is a small child, he has an assured source of income. Boy and elephant will grow up together, and the elephant will obey and work only for his boy."

"Northern Thailand was where you went this week, wasn't it?"

"Yes."

"I hope your patient wasn't serious."

"Just an appendectomy. He was with an advisory mission in a remote area where there wasn't a hospital, so we picked him up and brought him to Bangkok. But enough of this shop talk, we came down here to ski, and I see our boat coming."

"When did you arrange for it?" Wendy asked, recognizing the boat and driver who had taken her skiing that morning, followed by the exuberant Tahn shouting and waving from the end of the tow line.

"Before I came down to the beach. A half hour skiing is enough for me, so I always let the boys have the other half hour," answered Erick returning Tahn's sweeping wave.

The boat pulled in to the hotel landing and Wendy climbed in as Tahn turned the skis over to Erick and climbed in beside her. The driver eased the boat smoothly away from the dock, and as the tow rope tightened, Erick rose gracefully on the skis in one fluid motion. The driver moved out into the harbor in a series of sweeping turns, Erick following behind as if man, skis, and rope were one—a piece of modern bronze sculpture.

Then it was Wendy's turn. She mentally reviewed Tahn's instructions: hold back and let the boat bring you up—balance with your knees and ankles. She managed to stay up for about ten seconds before losing her balance and toppling into the water. She hadn't learned to ski, but she had been spared having Erick watch her first awkward attempts.

Erick looked suspiciously from Wendy to Tahn, as if her performance had been better than might be expected for a first trial on water skis. "You learn fast," he commented.

Tahn grinned and ducked his head.

After another beautiful performance by Erick and another faltering one by Wendy, Erick once more donned the skis and told the driver, "Give us a circle tour of the harbor and then head back to the boat dock."

There were beautiful yachts and colorful junks tied up in the harbor, but Wendy only had eyes for Erick as he skimmed the water with effortless grace. She came back from her preoccupation with a start as they coasted in to the boat dock.

Tahn's brothers were waiting on the dock, balancing a bicycle between them. Tahn climbed on the seat, the youngest brother mounted the handlebars, and the third stood behind Tahn on two pegs which extended from the socket of the rear wheel. "Their family can only afford one bicycle," Erick explained as the three boys rode off waving, undaunted by their precarious balance.

"Would you like to change for dinner?" Erick asked.

"Sounds good after that workout," Wendy agreed.

Erick had not yet returned when Wendy strolled out into the garden wearing the pareu print she had bought in Tahiti. She wasn't sure why she had selected that dress. Perhaps she was trying to recapture the magic of those earlier evenings.

Wendy sat on a bench by the children's playground, her position partly screened by a softly scented jasmine so that she could watch the games without making the children self-conscious. Wendy thought she had never seen such beautiful children. One little girl—a child of about three or four—seemed a doll come to life.

As if drawn by Wendy's concentration, the child came skipping over to the bench. "Hello, what's your name?" Wendy asked, regretting that she had not yet learned the language well enough to ask in Thai.

"Urai," the child answered, pressing her chubby fingers together and bowing in greeting.

"My name is Wendy. How old are you?" Wendy continued, testing whether the child understood English or always started a new encounter with her name.

"Free."

As Wendy tried to think of suitable words to continue the conversation, the child emitted a joyful shriek, "Daaady," and went flying across the lawn.

Wendy was stunned to see that the man who swooped Urai up and tossed her in the air was Erick. She had been prepared for a mysterious woman in Erick's life in Bangkok, but not a child.

The next few seconds seemed like an eternity to Wendy. Finally, her pulse began to beat again as a soft, musical voice called "Urai."

The beautiful Thai woman who came down the path had the same doll-like quality as Urai. "Erick!" she cried in surprise when she saw the two of them. She did not rush to him as Migin, Niki, and Wendy herself had done; instead she held out her hands in greeting.

Erick took her two small hands in his and kissed them gently. "You're looking lovely as ever, Sumnieng. How are things with you?"

"Things go well. I dance again at the restaurant—and then there is Urai."

The tenderness and pain evident between them made Wendy feel as if she had opened the wrong door, intruded on two people at a very private moment.

Sumnieng and Erick turned and went back up the path to the garden, Urai skipping and dancing between them as she clung tightly to Erick's hand. Wendy sat motionless until they were out of sight, lest any movement attract their attention. When she was sure she would not be seen, she ran blindly up the walk to the hotel, narrowly missing a waiter with a tray of drinks at the corner of the swimming pool.

When she reached the solitude of her room, Wendy looked down at her trembling hands, waiting for the burst of temper with which she usually met such frustration, but it did not come. Instead, she felt drained and empty. She slumped into a chair and sat motionless, searching her memory for some chance word anyone might have said which would provide a clue to the scene she had just witnessed. She could not say how long she sat there when her phone rang.

"Hi, I was afraid I might have missed you," said Erick, an odd defensive note in his voice. "I'm afraid I have bad news. There is an emergency at Nongkai, and the other pilots are all out on missions, so I've been called back. Sorry to desert you like this—I warned you pilots are a bad risk. We have to leave now. I'll call you when I get back."

Wendy was glad he hadn't waited for an answer; at the moment she was completely out of them. Erick's call had only added more questions: how had he been called back to Bangkok when she had seen him only minutes before walking in the garden with Sumnieng? Was it a slip when he said, "we have to leave now"? Or had he been trying to tell her that he was leaving with Sumnieng and Urai? She felt more abandoned than she had when Marvin failed to arrive for their wedding. The delightful resort of a few hours before had become a strange land where she was completely alone. Utterly desolated, she threw herself on the bed and cried. . . .

When it was over she felt better. She got up and washed her face in cold water. After all, Pattaya was one of Thailand's most popular tourist resorts, a place to be included by Personal World Tours, which meant there was work here for her to do. She put her notebook in her purse, brushed back a tumble of wayward curls, and headed resolutely down the path past the swimming pool.

CHAPTER SEVEN

Wendy spent the days following her return from Pattaya familiarizing herself with Bangkok and the places Personal World would want to include in their tours—the Royal Palace, beautiful and varied Buddhist temples, the floating markets, the silk factory, and gem shops. She was too busy by day and too tired at night to dwell on her personal problems; but without Erick people and places just didn't come alive as they had before.

When the phone rang Wednesday evening, Wendy restrained herself from racing to it like a teen-age girl.

"I hear you need tour guide," said Erick in a rich, playful Thai accent which sent a tingle through her.

"Do you have references?" she asked, joining in the game.

"Very fine references. I show you Thai restaurant

with dancing. The star is friend of mine," said Erick, continuing the imitation.

Remembering Erick's meeting with Sumnieng and her reference to dancing, Wendy had to concentrate on keeping her tone light as she replied, "What time does the tour start?"

"Tour bus arrive at seven o'clock," he answered and hung up. If he was going to offer any further explanation of his sudden departure from Pattaya, he obviously did not want to do it over the phone.

In spite of her stern admonitions, Wendy found it difficult to suppress her excitement as she dressed for their dinner date in the soft green silk dress the seamstress had finished for her just that afternoon. She told herself that the sparkle in her green eyes was just a complement of the color of the dress.

"I have a surprise for you." Erick greeted her with the enthusiasm of a child with a new toy and led her to the parking lot. "The new tour bus," he said, waving his hand grandly to indicate a small, battered green Toyota. "After Pattaya, I realized I had to have a car, and when one of the mechanics returning to the States offered to sell me this one, I jumped at the chance."

Wendy waited for a further explanation of what had happened at Pattaya, and what the incident had to do with owning a car, but Erick was engrossed with his new toy.

"At least it's the right color," he said, turning to look for a long moment into the depth of her eyes. "I call it shamrock because finding it was a piece of good luck."

"A Japanese shamrock?" Wendy giggled in spite of herself.

"You can find shamrocks in lots of odd corners of the world," he said, and abruptly turned his attention back to the car. When he started the engine, the purr of the motor belied its age. It had obviously been an object of loving care from a man who knew motors. As he skillfully maneuvered the little car through the confusion of Bangkok traffic, Erick drove with an ease Wendy had often observed in pilots.

They crossed the arching bridge of the Baan Thong Restaurant, and Wendy felt the change from bustling, modern Bangkok to ancient Siam. In the entry of the converted teak mansion they removed their shoes and received slippers from the attendant. A smiling hostess in a sarong led them up the broad, curving stairway covered with thick red carpeting. The dining room was filled with low, carved teak tables surrounded by wedge-shaped cushions for reclining. Three Americans were already seated at the table. Erick introduced the attractive girl with short honey-colored hair as Captain Jane Adams; a distinguished man with gray at the temples as Major Warren Sims; and a scholarly looking man with glasses as Captain Paul Hess.

When the introductions were completed, the Major indicated the places beside him for Wendy and Erick. "No wonder you've been hiding her," he said with approval. "How was the flight to Nongkai?"

"No problem with the flight. The boy was near shock and weakening when we got him in," Erick answered. "How is he?" he asked, turning to Jane.

"He responded to the serum, and should be all right in a few days," she answered.

"A boy from one of the hill tribes was bitten by a cobra," Erick explained to Wendy. "They used a primitive treatment instead of antitoxen, and when it didn't work a ranger asked us to go up and bring him in."

"We try to keep all areas supplied with anti-venom from the Pasteur Institute here in Bangkok, but there are some of the more remote hill tribes that still don't use it," Jane added.

"I hope you like Thai food," the Major said. "Here everything is served as if we were guests at a Thai banquet."

The waitress, carrying a teak tray filled with small, artistically arranged dishes, dropped gracefully to her knees beside the low table and began serving the colorful foods.

Crisp cubes of pork garnished with pineapple and green peppers, succulent baby shrimp with snow peas, and other combinations of tasty morsels of meat with crunchy vegetables reminded Wendy of San Francisco's Chinatown. Yet the subtle spices and the frequent use of ground peanuts made the colorfully arranged dishes distinctly Thai. There were so many different dishes, Wendy was hard-pressed to sample each of the inviting offerings. A pot of green tea kept hot by a brightly decorated caddy, and a plate of chilled fruit and melon completed the meal.

The waitress was just removing the fruit plate when the orchestra, which had played soft, hauntingly elusive music throughout dinner, began a more insistent beat, and the first group of elaborately costumed dancers appeared on stage. The dance depicted a mass battle scene from the epic Ramayana; not the entire story as the Balinese dancers had told it, but only the dramatic concluding scene. Monkeys and other animal characters wore fierce stylized masks beneath their towering headdresses. The dancers representing human characters did not wear masks, but kept their faces immobile except for their expressive eyes.

The polite applause which followed the number gave way to an enthusiastic reception as the next dancer, a soloist, appeared. Wendy immediately recognized Sumnieng, her lovely face framed by a towering gold and jeweled headdress. The heavy, jeweled brocade of her Siamese costume did not conceal the remarkable grace of her slender body as she began the ancient ceremonial dance.

Erick and his friends followed every subtle motion of her delicate hands and flashing eyes with rapt attention. The applause which followed Sumnieng's dance left no doubt that she had brought something special to the familiar ritual.

"She's marvelous," enthused Erick. "More polished and confident than when I saw her last."

"She has become one of Thailand's most talented dancers," replied the Major. "You will notice that most of the customers are not tourists but Thai. Many have come particularly to see Sumnieng dance. When Dhamak, the owner, gloats over his find, I am tempted to remind him of his reluctance to rehire a widow—it took a bit of arm twisting."

"An old specialty of yours, arm twisting, as I remember," prodded Erick.

"She makes me feel as ancient and graceless as a helicopter," complained Jane, whose trim figure, dynamic appeal, and quick, efficient movements belied both statements.

"Don't knock our trusted beast of burden," admonished Paul.

A comic monkey dance and a romantic duet preceded Sumnieng's next appearance. She performed the fingernail dance with long, curved, golden fingernails accenting the delicate expressive movements of her hands. Though the dance was sheer poetry in motion, it was Sumnieng's serene, beautiful eyes which riveted Wendy's attention. The applause was even more enthusiastic when the dance ended.

"I wish I could go backstage and tell her how much I enjoyed it," said Erick.

"Afraid not," answered the Major. To Wendy he explained, "Though classic Thai dances are no longer restricted to the temples and palaces, contact between dancers and spectators is not encouraged."

"I'm taking Urai to the zoo tomorrow," said Paul. "I'll give Sumnieng your compliments."

"With a whole squadron of American daddies, you'll spoil that child rotten in spite of Sumnieng's careful training," chided Jane.

"I've offered to cut the number to one," said Paul.

Erick too? Wendy wondered, recalling his meeting with Sumnieng in Pattaya.

"She's come a long way since Jimmy's death, but until she really finds herself again, I'm afraid those decisions will have to wait," said the Major.

"Did the Thompsons ever come to their senses and accept her and Urai?" asked Erick so quietly only the Major and Wendy could hear.

"She has heard nothing more from them. They still refuse to acknowledge that Jimmy was married, that she even exists."

A clash of cymbals brought the final victory dance to a close and the house lights came on. Wendy and Erick said good night to the others. The streets were almost deserted as Erick turned the small car out of the Baan Thong parking lot.

The Bangkok which Wendy knew as a modern, bustling city by day had become a starlit Oriental wonderland by night; roofs curling upward with carved monkeys on the tips; slender, spired temples gleaming white and gold in the moonlight. Even the neon signs winked back an exotic alphabet that looked more like music than words. Or was it the companion beside her who produced the magic?

"I'm afraid I'll have to renege again on that tour," said Erick as they approached Wendy's hotel. "I have to fly Jane and some antitoxin up to Nongkai tomorrow. The Major feels we should press our advantage while the people are still excited about the boy and the helicopter. Jane will spend the day teaching their medicine men how to adminster the serum."

"You mean medicine men like those with American Indian tribes?"

"These men are trained in ancient Chinese herbal medicine, but there is a good deal of superstition and ritual mixed in."

"Does Jane speak Thai?" Wendy asked.

"Well enough to give her demonstration in it," answered Erick, his voice reflecting respect for Jane's abilities. "But the hill tribes speak their own language. The Thai government will send an interpreter along. It's a joint project. I think she could do it in pantomime if she had to. It's a pretty sound international language if you are really trying to communicate."

"Pantomime is a language I'm getting pretty good at," laughed Wendy.

As Erick kissed her good night, Wendy forced herself to keep her response light and casual. There were so many questions left unanswered. Who was the girl in Bangkok Migin had spoken of? Was it pert, efficient Jane who was a part of his work—who shared so much of Erick's life? Or was it the beautiful, talented Sumnieng, cherished by all of them? Wendy felt as if she had come in during the second act of a play without knowing what had gone before, or quite what was going on now. At least the emergency at Nongkai had been real enough. She hated to admit to herself that she had questioned it.

CHAPTER EIGHT

Wendy slept restlessly, then lingered over breakfast, finding it hard to concentrate on completing her Bangkok program for Personal World Tours. The morning mail had arrived by the time she finished. The clerk handed her a thin envelope bearing Marvin's return address. The short note read:

Dear Wendy,

Dr. Pridi has asked me to present our findings at the International Rice Research Conference at their headquarters in Bangkok on the 15th. It is more good fortune than I had hoped for to have my two favorite projects in the same place. You will still be in Bangkok, won't you? I do want to make you understand how I feel about you.

Love,
Marvin

It seemed ironic that the man who couldn't manage to travel a hundred miles to marry her should follow her halfway around the world. But that wasn't really true; he was in fact coming to see Dr. Pridi, the same man whose visit had taken precedence over their wedding. And Marvin didn't have to take much trouble to get himself here; the laboratory's efficient secretary, Mrs. Jenkins, would have arranged for his passport, typed his notes, made his reservations—done everything but pack his clothes. That was where Wendy would have come in if they had been married. She wrinkled her upturned nose, but her anger and frustration were gone. She wasn't sure what feelings remained. You really should feel something about a man you were within hours of marrying, Wendy told herself.

She took her appointment calendar from her purse. She was forced to face the question she had been avoiding: when was she going on to Hong Kong? Was she staying in Bangkok for the snatches of time she could be with Erick? Was her work here really finished?

Avoiding an answer, she began drawing up charts of the itineraries for the various tours. They seemed quite complete. She could of course check on side trips to Chiengmai and the hill country. They sounded so fascinating when Erick and his friends talked about them. She could fly up for two days and still be back to ski on the weekend—and maybe go to Hong Kong Monday. She wasn't planning to leave Bangkok soon to avoid Marvin, she told herself.

There was a light tap on the door. It was Tahn. He raised his familiar red cap in greeting.

"Tahn, come in," she invited.

"I must make big hurry, or I will be late at the temple. I would like for you to come to my house on the night of the new moon—that is in five days, for party when I become Buddhist monk."

"I thought you were going to be a boatman," Wendy answered, surprised by the announcement.

"In three months I will be a boatman, but first I will be a monk. I am the oldest son, and to be a monk will gain much merit for my family."

"I'd love to come," said Wendy, not quite understanding, but eager to meet Tahn's family and friends and share such an occasion. "Is Erick coming?"

"Of course, he is my special friend."

"And Miss Jane?"

"Yes, she is good friend too." A quizzical look crossed Tahn's face. He turned abruptly and left, pausing for a familiar wave of the cap as he bounded out into the courtyard. Wendy felt an odd mixture of pleasure at having been invited by Tahn to such an important occasion, and doubt because she could not reconcile her view of him with this new role. However, the invitation did provide the answer to her immediate problem. She would stay in Bangkok another week and check on potential side trips.

The silvery crescent of the new moon rose slowly above the horizon as Wendy and Erick turned off the main highway onto the wagon road which led to

Tahn's village. Wendy read the ancient promise of new beginnings in such a heavenly sign. As they approached the village, it was easy to identify Tahn's house. Colored lights were strung in the trees in front of the small house set on stilts. Sounds of music and laughter came from inside.

As Erick and Wendy climbed the stairs, Tahn greeted them with a deep *wai* in place of his usual wave and "hi!" "Miss Jane does not come?" he asked, disappointment in his voice.

"There was an emergency at the hospital," answered Erick. "She had to work late. She'll be here when she finishes."

Wendy and Erick were presented to Tahn's parents, grandparents, aunts, uncles, brothers, sisters, and other relatives and friends. Three large silk cushions had obviously been saved for the American guests. As soon as they were seated, beautiful girls in *pasin*, the colorful batik sarongs, served Wendy and Erick nuts and fruits, arranged on lacquer trays in a colorful mosaic of tempting delicacies.

"I am Tawee," said a schoolboy settling himself on the cushion beside Erick, which had been left vacant by Jane's absence. Wendy recognized the boy as the brother who had ridden on the handlebars of the group bicycle when Tahn went to Pattaya. The boy asked the English textbook questions he had learned in school about Erick's family and where he was from. Erick answered with as near textbook answers as possible. Only the reply that he was from Wisconsin seemed to bother the boy, who apparently believed from the tourists he had met that all Americans were from California, New York, or Texas. With the formalities completed, Tawee came to the most important matter. "While Tahn is a monk, can I be your lookout boy?" he asked.

"Can you shout 'lookout' very loud?" teased Erick.

"Lookout," the boy shouted so loud that the startled guests turned toward him, and then began to roar with laughter at his embarrassment.

"I'm sure that will do just fine," said Erick. Can you meet me in Pattaya Saturday morning?"

"Yes, I can pedal a long way," said Tawee, now promoted to the seat of the bicycle as well as the job of lookout.

Tawee was replaced on the cushion beside Erick by three progressively younger boys testing their mastery of the required school English. Wendy was amazed at Erick's patience and good humor as he carefully repeated the answers.

The music they had heard when arriving began again, provided by gongs suspended in a round frame and a drum. The guests sang along with the music. Two very old ladies wearing bright *pasin* sat in a corner pounding betel nuts. Occasionally they puckered their scarlet, betel-stained lips and joined in an ancient chant.

Then it was time for a solo. The drummer passed the drum to the guest sitting next to him. The man sang a simple tune while he beat out the rhythm on the drum. The next man to receive the drum collaborated with his neighbor by playing a rapid beat resembling a jig, while the other man performed a monkey dance. The round of singing and dancing continued until the drum was passed to Erick. "Would you care to join me, or do you want to solo?" he asked Wendy with a touch of mischief.

"Wherever thou leadest," she responded.

Erick began a familiar rhythm and his rich baritone filled the room with, "I Left My Heart in San Francisco." As Wendy joined in, she wondered if he sang of the lonely servicemen in the Orient whose last glimpse of the United States had been the Golden Gate, or whether he was expressing a more personal message.

"Bravo!" applauded Jane, who had entered as they were finishing.

The entertainment paused for a new round of introductions before Jane was seated beside Erick. While the traditional refreshments were still being served, a lovely, shy girl Wendy had noticed hovering in the background all evening moved quietly beside Jane and sat at her feet. "You are a nurse?" she asked with awe.

During the singing and dancing the young girls stayed on one side of the room making delicate paper flowers that would be presented at the temple the next day. Now several of them sat beside Jane to work and listen to her conversation with Tahn's sister, Kokay.

The entertainment resumed, first with community singing and then with more solos. When the drum completed the circle and came to Jane, she handed it to Erick. As he began the familiar beat of "When the Saints Come Marching In," Jane took a folded paper nurse's cap from her purse and pinned it on her head at a rakish angle, then slowly pulled out a long honey-comb tissue paper vaccination needle. She charged and pranced about the room feinting and jabbing her oversized needle at the guests, who clapped in time to the drum beat and shouted their approval. It was a routine she and Erick had obviously used before. Wendy could not deny feeling envious of the esteem with which the guests regarded the American nurse, and of the unspoken communication between Jane and Erick.

Group singing and dancing continued. "We have to drive back to Pattaya so we must go," Erick told Tahn. "Good luck."

"You will be back tomorrow?" Tahn asked anxiously.

"Oh, yes, I wouldn't miss the chance to see you speechless all that time," Erick teased his young friend.

"The silence before being presented at the temple gives the novice a chance to appear more wise than he really is, and not half so scared," answered Tahn in the stage whisper of a conspirator.

When they returned to Tahn's village the following morning, Wendy could scarcely believe that the serious young man with the shaved head and wearing white robes was the lively, fun-loving Tahn who had taught her to water-ski. Nine monks in traditional saffron robes chanted from a scroll of Buddhist writings. The ordination was scheduled for noon, when the monks at the *wat* would have finished their last meal of the day.

"Tahn would be pleased to ride in your car—our family does not have a car, or horse, or elephant," Tawee told Erick.

Erick ceremoniously opened the door and Tahn, holding a candle and a flower between his hands, slid into the front seat. Tawee seated himself beside Tahn to give directions, since Tahn was not allowed to speak. An awkward pause followed, which Jane broke by asking so all could hear, "Wendy, would you like to ride with me?"

With the protocol problem solved, Tahn's father, grandfather, and eldest uncle seated themselves in the back of Erick's car. In the meantime, Jane bowed to Tahn's mother, who did not speak English, and gestured toward her car. Tahn's grandmother was invited in a similar manner. Then, while Tahn's eldest aunt and the wife of his eldest uncle each smiled shyly in anticipation, Jane turned to Tahn's sister Kokay and said, "Why don't you ride with me, and we can talk more about being a nurse?"

Kokay lowered her eyes and nodded acceptance, the trace of a smile on her lips.

Wendy suspected that Jane had planned this gesture of equality from the time she had declined Erick's offer to ride with them from Pattaya to the village and instead drove her own car. It turned out to be a two-edged gesture—it had given the women of the family equal transportation with the men riding in Erick's car ahead of them; it had also given Jane's new-found protegée, Kokay, the prestige of the mature women of the family.

The cars were followed by *samlors* for the aunts—

not the motorized *samlors* of Bangkok, but rickshaws pulled by a bicycle. The younger members of the family and some of the older ones rode bicycles, the boys piling up in every available combination. Tahn's younger brother had advanced from the spokes of the rear wheel of the family bicycle to the seat, since the older boys were riding in Erick's car. The rest of the family and friends walked behind the bicycles. The marching group was preceded by the drummer from the evening's festivities. He kept up a lively beat and the guests sang as the procession wound through the streets to the temple.

When they arrived at the temple, the procession was reversed. The drummer and a guest playing a flute led, followed by the marchers, the bicyclists, Tahn's immediate family, and finally Tahn himself, carried on Tawee's shoulders, while a younger brother held an umbrella over his head to shield him from the sun. They marched around the *wat* three times and entered.

Two rows of monks, seated facing each other, formed an aisle on the platform in front of the image of Buddha. As the procession entered, the men seated themselves on the floor on the right side of the temple, the women on the left. Tawee motioned for Erick, Jane, and Wendy to join him in the center of the room, seated so that he and Erick were on the right side of Wendy and Jane.

Tahn approached the abbot, who was sitting in front of the huge statue, and repeated a chant three times.

"He's speaking Pali, the ancient language, asking to

be admitted to the brotherhood," Tawee whispered.

Wendy was embarrassed by the distraction, but other spectators also talked among themselves, perhaps because few of them understood Pali.

The abbot answered in a long chant. "He is being told the rules against killing, stealing, adultery, lying, and drinking alcohol," their self-appointed interpreter told them. "He is also told that monks may not eat after midday or wear any type of ornament."

Two monks gave Tahn his saffron robes and a large rice bowl, and went to help him change. When Tahn returned in his yellow robes, he was asked a set of ritual questions by his teacher, the abbot, and each monk in the room. To each question he gave the same ritual answers.

"They ask if he is human, and if he is an adult male," Tawee explained.

After more questions, answers, and instructions, Tahn announced the name in Pali by which he would be known, and the ordination was concluded. The paper flowers and other decorations were presented to the abbot for the temple. Tahn's friends gave him gifts of the few items a monk is allowed to possess: books of the Buddha's teachings, candles, soap, an umbrella. A slim, leather-bound volume of the *Jataka Tales* lay beside Tahn's rice bowl. When he spied it, Tahn picked it up, ran his fingers appreciatively over the embossed leather, and turned a broad smile toward Erick, who made a slight *wai* in return. Taking Wendy's hand, Erick led her out of the temple.

"Well, what do you think of our boy?" he asked.

"He seemed so serious, so capable. It was a side I

wouldn't have suspected," she answered. "But I shudder at the thought of him having to beg for food in the streets, even if it is only for three months."

"The monks don't really beg. They collect the donations from the faithful each morning. These gifts of food are the lay person's opportunity to earn merit. The monk isn't allowed to thank the giver because that would reduce the merit. Instead, the donor thanks the monk for accepting the offering."

Resuming her place beside Erick in his car, Wendy thought that Tahn wasn't the only one who had shown a surprising new depth.

Leaving their hosts to finish the traditional celebration, Wendy and Erick drove back to Pattaya. The inviting cool of the breaking surf was the perfect answer to the heat of the afternoon. They romped and frolicked in the waves as if to wash away memories of their last visit to Pattaya, which had ended so abruptly.

The new moon was just rising over the horizon like a small silver sail when they headed back to Bangkok. An almost mystical serenity hung over the ancient land. The highway, so jammed with pedestrians, bicycles, carts, and buses during the day, was nearly deserted. Crickets competed with the sound of distant temple bells to provide evening vespers. With Erick's hand gently covering hers, Wendy felt completely at peace.

At a lookout point on the crest of a hill Erick stopped the car. Joining the sliver of a moon, the stars twinkled so brightly in the velvet sky that it seemed to Wendy they could reach up and touch them. In the broad valley below them, the twinkling lights were repeated. Those gliding down the inky outline of the river were the torches of night fishermen. Flickering lights outlining the river were lanterns in houses which rose on stilts along its banks. The scene seemed untouched by time.

Erick and Wendy watched it in silence, and then his arm around her shoulders gently turned her toward him and he kissed her. It was not the flaming, passionate kiss of the night of the full moon in Bali; it was a lingering kiss of tenderness and promise.

He raised his head and looked at her for a long moment, then he ran his fingers gently through the tumble of soft curls which framed her face. He kissed the tip of her perky nose and again, gently, her trembling lips. Desperately she longed to share her life with this man whose many changing moods captured her own.

CHAPTER NINE

Wendy closed her eyes and leaned back from the writing table. It had been a busy day—she always seemed to try to cram the days too full when Erick was flying. It can't be Erick, she told herself as the phone jolted her back into action, but the tingle in her fingers as she reached for it contradicted the logic of her thought.

"Hello?"

"Hello, Wendy, this is Marvin. I came a couple of days early so I could see you before the conference." His voice sounded a long way off although the connection was perfectly clear.

"Marvin, where are you?" Wendy answered, feeling like a schoolgirl who, after having failed to work out an assigned problem, was being called on to recite.

"At the Dusit Thani—our conference will be held here. Will you have dinner with me?"

Wendy was tempted to say that she had already eaten, but the hour was too early, and it was her habit to tackle a problem head-on. "Fine," she answered, hoping he hadn't heard the deep breath that preceded her decision to accept.

"Pick you up in half an hour," Marvin said, and hung up before she could change her mind.

As she replaced the receiver and stood staring down at it, reluctant to get ready for her date, Wendy smiled at the thought of Marvin ever being two days early for anything.

She glanced at herself in the mirror. The well-designed, beige linen dress she had just put on suited a quiet dinner alone but was hardly appropriate for a dinner date. She shrugged, and added a pale green Thai silk scarf at the V neckline. Did Marvin like for her to wear green to bring out the color of her eyes? She couldn't seem to remember.

"You're looking well," Marvin greeted her as she walked across the lobby to meet him.

"So are you," she answered. That was certainly an understatement, she thought. His shirt and tie were carefully coordinated with his expensively tailored suit. His dark hair was longer than when she had seen him last, styled in a continental manner. Gone was the scholarly look she used to tease him about; only the tip of his dark-rimmed glasses peaked from his breast pocket. His choices had obviously been made to impress a young lady, not a gathering of scientists. Must mean that I am the top priority project, at least for the moment, she concluded, smiling at the thought.

Encouraged by her smile, he continued. "I've made reservations at the Starlight Room; is that all right?"

Wendy would have preferred any other place to the one where she and Erick had gone on her first night in Bangkok, but she answered. "It's very nice."

Marvin asked the doorman to hail a taxi and directed the driver to the Dusit Thani. "You should hail the cab yourself and agree on the price with the driver before you get in," Wendy told him.

"I know, I've read that in the guide book, but I just can't," Marvin answered.

The cab took them to the porticoed carriage entrance below which the baby elephant stood in the center of a small group of children. Wendy ridiculously felt as if she had passed an old friend without saying hello.

They took the express elevator to the tower. Wendy was relieved when Marvin did not stop at the panorama window from which she had first become fascinated by Bangkok, but turned instead toward the dining room.

"I haven't congratulated you on your selection for the conference," Wendy said when they were seated.

"I was pleased to be asked," Marvin admitted. "We are making important progress in the Green Revolution, as they call it over here. Our new high-yield hybrid and those of some of the other researchers should increase the world's rice supply fifty percent in the next three years."

Wendy again felt pride in the importance of Marvin's work and his dedication to it.

The waiter interrupted then, and Marvin ordered his usual steak well-done. At least that hasn't changed, Wendy thought. She compromised on the herbed roast chicken rather than the more exotic Thai dishes she and Erick would have ordered. She imagined that Erick and Jane would be guests tonight at a dinner in their honor somewhere in the hills near Nongkai.

"Have you visited any of the rice fields near Bangkok?" Marvin's voice brought her wandering thoughts back to their dinner.

"No, I've only seen them from the road. They do look good, though."

"Some of the best in the Orient. Would you like to visit them tomorrow, then we could do some sightseeing?"

Wendy hesitated, searching for an excuse.

"It's the only free time I'll have before the conference starts." His eyes pleaded for her to accept.

"I guess there's nothing I can't postpone," she admitted.

Encouraged by her acceptance, Marvin spent the rest of dinner giving her a detailed report on the progress of his work. On the way back to her hotel, his hand covered hers and pressed it gently. She started to withdraw it, but decided that would be childish when he was trying so hard to please her.

"See you at eight," he said at her door. "Good night." He pressed her hand again, turned, and left. Wendy was grateful that he had not tried to kiss her. Anger and the hurt had left her long ago, but so had whatever feelings she had mistaken for love.

Marvin was waiting for her when Wendy crossed the lobby a few minutes before eight the next morning. This is new, she thought, remembering all the times she had waited for him—including that last embarrassing wait.

"I'm so glad you decided to come," he greeted her.

They took a taxi to the International Rice Institute. A tour bus was parked in front of the building, and small groups of men and women of different nationalities gathered on the sidewalk. If Wendy had realized the visit to the rice fields was a tour of the delegates, she would not have accepted. Still, it was an opportunity to study the organization of professional interest tours. She sighed quietly and followed Marvin toward the others. The guide was just announcing the loading of the bus.

They visited three rice fields. At each one, a member of the Thai delegation explained the planting and cultivating techniques, varieties, and yield, and answered questions posed in several languages. Marvin and the other delegates diligently took notes. Wendy had to keep reminding herself how important increased rice yields were to the people of Asia, as she smiled politely and nodded to wives of other delegates. It was almost noon when they returned to Bangkok.

"Would you like to take a boat trip on the *klongs* to

see the floating market?" Wendy asked Marvin as they finished their lunch at the cafeteria of the Rice Institute.

"You know what I like. Whatever you think would be interesting," answered Marvin. In the old, familiar pattern Wendy found herself making arrangements which she hoped would suit him.

"After being with all those people this morning, let's take a boat by ourselves rather than join a tour," she suggested.

The beaming smile Marvin gave her at this suggestion made Wendy hope he hadn't misunderstood her reasons for selecting a boat by themselves. It was part of her personalized tour planning to always balance independent shopping and sightseeing against group tours.

The boatman took them across the swirling, muddy Chao Phya River to the Wat Arun, Temple of the Dawn. Wendy was as enchanted as she had been the first time she saw its towers glimmering like jewels, as the sunlight reflected off the walls made of broken table pottery set in flower patterns. The boatman tied the canopied motor launch to the temple dock, and the three of them climbed the gentle incline to the temple. The boatman lit a prayer stick before the huge, gilded image of Buddha, and pressed his palms together in silent prayer.

The smell of incense hung in the air, and Wendy found the atmosphere both peaceful and exotic. She glanced at Marvin, who was carefully examining the imposing figure, the offerings of food and flowers, the massive teakwood beams and supports against the whitewashed walls. Wendy thought Erick would have been fascinated by the people in the temple; Marvin found the temple itself more interesting. Marvin began to move toward the door, and the others followed him.

They paused on the dock to watch the colorful panorama passing on the river, one of Thailand's main avenues of commerce. A constant stream of small, flat-bottomed boats passed them, carrying fruits and vegetables to Bangkok—peanuts, coconuts, oranges, papayas, mangos, and bananas. Wendy had never seen so many bananas. Some of the boats had umbrellas or low, curved covers to shade the passengers from the tropical sun. The boats were steered from the rear with a long pole.

"Seems like another world, doesn't it?" said Wendy. The driver carefully steered the boat through the main channel so as not to disturb mothers bathing their children in the muddy water in front of their houses perched on stilts out over the water.

Marvin only nodded as he reached out and covered her hand with his. He seemed to be searching for something to say, or perhaps the right words to say it, when a small, flat-bottomed canoe pulled alongside their motor launch and a boy held out a tray of carved teakwood figures. Marvin waved him away impatiently.

"This isn't exactly the way I pictured a river cruise," complained Marvin.

"Does the way these people live bother you?" Wendy asked.

"It seems so unsanitary," he answered, and Wendy

remembered the antiseptic sterility of the laboratory where Marvin worked. Yet the whole purpose of his experiments was to provide more food for people like these.

"You've been here more than two weeks," Marvin continued. "Do you really like it here?"

There seemed no way that Wendy could make Marvin understand about Sumnieng, Urai, Tahn and his family; or about wanting to communicate to the people on the tours she planned the feeling she had for Thailand and its people. At that moment she realized that she wanted to specialize in Thailand. Because of Erick? the little pixie voice inside her asked. She staunchly denied it to herself. There was something about these serene, smiling people and their ancient culture that struck a responsive chord in her. She only regretted that the country was no longer called Siam, a name which for her tied the present to the past.

"When are you coming home?" Marvin's impatient voice interrupted her thoughts.

He sounds like a father talking to a college student spending a summer vacation abroad, she thought. Marvin had never taken her work very seriously.

Apparently noting the flash of annoyance in her green eyes, he became contrite. "I guess I had no right to ask that. What I've really been trying to ask since the night I arrived is . . . can you forgive me?"

"That happened a long time ago."

"I think I sensed that when I saw you coming across the lobby to meet me, your eyes as soft as the silk scarf you were wearing."

Wendy remembered how precise and observant

Marvin could be when he really devoted his attention to a project—or a girl.

"Then perhaps we can go back and start again, just as I do when I make a mistake or grow careless about my research projects?" he asked hopefully.

Wendy was startled that he had picked up her thoughts, comparing his approach to her with his approach to one of his scientific projects.

"I'm not sure it would be that easy," she answered.

"But I can try, starting as soon as the conference ends."

As if on signal, a small boat loaded with flowers pulled beside the launch, and Marvin turned to examine them.

"I'll take the best white orchid," he said, indicating a clump of small white dendrobiums.

For her wedding gown . . . Wendy's mind completed the familiar line from the song. She turned away as the memory of her wedding day caused a shiver to run through her, in spite of the heat of the summer day.

When the launch returned to the main Chao Phya River dock, she declined Marvin's invitation to dinner, saying, "It's been a long day." She had just begun to realize how long.

A cool evening breeze had sprung up by the time she reached her hotel. Her decision to choose Thailand as her special interest in the new tour program gave direction to her plans, which she felt had been drifting, and lifted her spirits as much as the change in the weather. After a light supper of colorful Thai dishes of native fruits and nuts, she returned to her room to review the information she had collected for tours in Thailand. She searched for ways to include more person-to-person contact with the Thai people.

The next day she went back to Timland, the park on the outskirts of Bangkok where Erick had taken her when she first arrived. She took more detailed notes about the representative work and culture of Thailand that was assembled there. The dancers were students from the Royal Dance Academy—young, graceful, and well-practiced in their roles, but lacking the polish of Sumnieng and her group. The Thai boxers were also young, and engaged each other with flying feet, fists, heads, their whole bodies. They fought with great gusto and good humor, but an occasional jolting blow would produce a burst of temper. Both boys and girls showed the same exuberance fighting with swords and bamboo poles. She was fascinated by women who wove delicate fabrics of Thai silk, and by men who painstakingly carved exquisite teakwood figures.

Best of all, she liked watching the elephants work, a throwback to her childhood enchantment with circus elephants, she told herself. These were not like the baby elephants of the Dusit Thani or the one on which she had ridden at Pattaya. They were huge working animals who felled, hauled, and floated teak logs in unquestioning obedience to the elephant boys who tended them.

The snakes in the serpentarium made her think of the work Jane and Erick were doing. The memory of swaying cobras remained with Wendy that evening as she waited for Erick's return from Nongkai. Her work, which had been going so well, bogged down. She tried to read some of the tales of the Ramayana to better understand Thai dancing and drama, but found herself unable to concentrate.

It was almost eleven o'clock when she gave up waiting for Erick's phone call and started preparing for bed. She heard the soft plop of the late edition of the English language newspaper outside her door—a courtesy which the hotel supplied its English-speaking guests.

Collecting the paper, she dropped it on her dressing table and picked up her hairbrush. As she vigorously brushed her thick tumble of soft brown curls, a routine for which she had found little time recently, she glanced at the headlines. Near the bottom of the front page she read:

PLANE WITH INJURED BOY MISSING

Chiengmai—A fourteen-year-old boy working in the teak forest . . . leg crushed by a falling tree . . . picked up by an American medical-evac helicopter from Bangkok . . .

The hairbrush stopped in mid-stroke, slipped from her limp fingers, and fell unnoticed to the floor as her mind screamed in stunned protest: Erick is missing!

CHAPTER TEN

Too numb to cry, Wendy stared back at her reflection in the dressing-table mirror with unseeing eyes. Her senses had ceased to function. She was roused from her stupor by a gentle tapping on her door. Like a person coming out of a trance, she went to answer it.

Dressed in the simple black skirt and white blouse of the peasants, Sumnieng stood with her eyes lowered in the manner of Oriental women. Her gleaming black hair was pulled into a coil at the nape of her slender neck. Simple and artless in dress and manner, she appeared to Wendy even more beautiful than she was in her glamorous dance costumes.

"Sumnieng! Come in. I'm sorry, I mean Mrs. Thompson."

"It's been a long time since anyone called me Mrs. Thompson. It is good to remember, but please call me Sumnieng. I have grown used to having just one name professionally. It is an ancient custom in our country." Looking from Wendy's drawn face to the newspaper on the dresser, she continued more slowly. "I see you already have the bad news. I hoped to be here when you heard." She held out her hand to Wendy.

Sumnieng declined the chair Wendy offered in favor of the large floor cushion on which she sat in the modest native fashion with her feet tucked under her. Wendy plopped cross-legged on the other fat silk cushion. The vision of a helicopter caught in her mind and caused a choking in her throat, which she attempted to hide behind the routines of hospitality. "Can I order you some tea or a cool drink?" she asked.

"Tea would only taste salty from our unshed tears as we wait," Sumnieng answered. "I have learned much about waiting and about being alone. That is why I have come to share with you the wait for word of Erick."

"How did you know about me?"

"In Pattaya I heard Erick telephone you from Paul's cottage after the Major called them back to Bangkok. I should have had the courage to go see you because I knew you were all alone in a strange place. But I did not know you were in love with Erick until the night you came with him to see me dance."

"You are very perceptive. When you are dancing you don't look like you are aware of anything else in the world."

"It is because I remember the joy of a woman's first love that I can read the look in your eyes."

Wendy started to protest, but she realized that Sumnieng was right. Erick was the first man, the only man she had ever truly loved.

Following her memory, Sumnieng continued. "My parents died when I was a child, and Jimmy was my whole life, my whole family. When he was killed, his parents in America would not accept his Thai wife, his unborn child. He was afraid there would be problems, that was why he did not tell them about me, about our marriage. He said when they met me everything would be all right. He was going to take me to America to meet his parents when my papers were ready. I was so alone, so lost when he died." Sumnieng's voice faltered.

Wendy could not look at the other girl lest she lose control of the tears she was so desperately blinking back.

"Jimmy's friends became my family," Sumnieng began again more slowly. "Tom and Mike, the Major, Jane, but most of all Erick, who had been Jimmy's best friend. He did all of the things that the oldest brother does in a Thai family—took care of the necessary arrangements, filled out all the papers. For the army there are so many. And he talked to me about my baby, and about her being very special because Jimmy and I had been so much in love. When Urai was born, Erick and Jane took me to the hospital, stayed with me all the time."

Engrossed as she was in Sumnieng's story, Wendy could not help note that, as always, it had been Erick and Jane together.

After a pause, Sumnieng continued. "The other

women in the hospital room could not understand. Each of these American officers would come to see me, and make funny noises for Urai and talk about what a beautiful baby she was, as if each one was her father. The sadness about Jimmy was always there, but Urai would not be without family as I was when my parents died. I would be able to keep her and raise her, and she would have her American daddies to spoil her. Jane was like an older sister to me."

Wendy recalled Jane complaining about how the American daddies were spoiling Urai.

"Sometimes when they came, Jimmy's friends joked too much, and laughed too much, and tried too hard to make me smile. I knew they were troubled. First it was Tom when he and Migin were to be married. I knew he was thinking how it would be for her if something happened to him like it did to Jimmy. Finally he decided to leave the army, but I think he is happy with the resort and diving and his boats. He always loved boats and they were part of Migin's life as they were of his."

"Did you meet Migin?" Wendy asked.

"No. Tom showed me pictures of her, and talked so much about her I feel I know her."

"I met Migin and Tom in Tahiti," said Wendy. "They're wonderful people, and seemed very happy."

"I'm glad," said Sumnieng. "Was that where you met Erick?"

"Yes, at their resort," answered Wendy, remembering with longing the happy, carefree days she and Erick had spent at their island retreat.

"When Tom and Migin were married, Erick went to

their wedding. Tom wanted him to leave the army and go into business with them, but Erick came back. Like Jimmy, Erick felt the work here was very important, helping the Thai government bring medical care and health programs to the remote villages."

"Are you in love with Erick?" Wendy finally blurted the question which had been nagging at her since the day she had been an unseen witness to their reunion in Pattaya.

"I have spoken English since I was a child in a mission school, but sometimes there are things which I find difficult to explain," answered Sumnieng. "You say you love your parents, your family, but that you are in love with your husband, your lover. In Thai the words are different, it is not so confusing. I love Erick like the older brother whose place he has taken for me. I love the Major as the father he has tried to be, but I am not in love with them like Jimmy."

"What about Paul?" Wendy asked, recalling his avowed interest in marrying Sumnieng.

Sumnieng lowered her eyes and hesitated several minutes before answering. "Paul is different. He was not a friend of Jimmy's. He did not come to Thailand when they did; he was Jimmy's replacement. But he says he does not want to take Jimmy's place with me. He says Jimmy and I were young lovers like the song in the play about the English woman Anna and our King when our country was still called Siam. Paul says that after so much sorrow and so much hard work and being alone, I have matured—that we would share a different kind of love."

Wendy knew that for Sumnieng no one could ever

replace her first love, and that for her too, no one could ever replace her love for Erick.

Like a person weighing both sides of a problem, Sumnieng continued, "I do not know. Paul knows I could never marry anyone whose family would not accept me and Urai. His mother wrote me a beautiful letter. She said they have no daughter, and would be very happy to have me for one, and to have Urai for their grandchild. Her letter made me very happy. I carry it with me." Her hand went to her waistband where a small silk purse was fastened in Thai custom.

"I did not mean to ask personal questions about you and Paul," said Wendy.

"It is to share with you as a friend that I have come," answered Sumnieng, "but it is you who have helped me see things more clearly. Perhaps you have helped me more than I have helped you."

"You have given me what I needed," said Wendy. "You have helped me understand what Erick and his friends are doing, how they feel about their work and about each other. Most of all, when I needed someone, I was not alone, even though speaking of these things brings back painful memories for you."

"For a few bad minutes, this is true. Then I know it is different. Greedy, angry men with hate in their hearts shot down Jimmy's helicopter as he tried to rescue wounded men, and he was lost for nothing. Erick flew his helicopter into dangerous mountains to help an injured boy. It was something he chose to do because it was important to him. But we must not think that Erick is dead. Finding people lost at sea or in remote mountains is part of the American squadron's work here. When it is light, all the American planes and helicopters in Thailand will be looking for Erick, and all the villagers they have helped will be looking too."

The mention of daylight made Wendy realize with a start how late it was. Time had begun to have significance again. She turned to the other girl with concern.

"Sumnieng, it is late and you have been working. You must be very tired."

"That is of no matter, but for Urai I must return. Even though she cannot tell time, if she awakens very late at night and I am not there, she becomes frightened. Perhaps it is because she senses that the housekeeper is worried. My house is very small, but will you come home with me so you will not be alone?"

"Thank you, no. This is where Erick expects me to be. If there is word of him, I should be here. I'll be all right now."

"I think American women are very brave," said Sumnieng as she rose to leave.

Wendy put her arms around the tiny dancer in a warm embrace that seemed to both startle and please her. She was reminded again of the great inner strength of Thai women beneath their doll-like beauty.

As the door closed softly behind Sumnieng, Wendy crumpled onto the bed and the long pent-up tears came in a great flood—for Sumnieng, for herself, for all women whose men lead lives of constant danger.

CHAPTER ELEVEN

Slowly the tears subsided, leaving Wendy feeling empty, emotionally exhausted. She sank into a deep, troubled sleep. Some time later she was jarred awake by the ringing of the phone. She catapulted out of bed, her whole being keyed to that sound. She snatched up the phone, saying "hello!" before the receiver had reached her ear.

"Good morning, this is Marvin," said the overly cheery voice.

Wendy steadied herself against the edge of the bed as a wave of disappointment swept over her. If there was a prize for bad timing, Marvin would certainly win it.

"Can you have breakfast with me? I have to see you." When she didn't answer, he continued, "It's awfully important."

If she was home, she would probably have cleaned

her apartment or done some other routine job to keep busy, but with no such occupation, perhaps listening to Marvin would be some distraction from the endless waiting which stretched ahead of her.

"All right. Here in the hotel coffee shop in half an hour. I'm expecting an important phone call, and they can page me there."

As she hung up the phone, Wendy wondered if there was really any chance of her receiving a call.

A brisk shower washed away most of the external evidence of the painful hours she had spent. As she crossed to her dressing table, the newspaper headlines about the missing helicopter leaped out at her, receded, then blurred like a vision under water. She opened a drawer and dropped the paper into it, not wanting the maid to throw away even this painful reminder of Erick. She retrieved her hairbrush from the floor where it had fallen the night before, but unwilling to resume the interrupted brushing, ran a comb briskly through her hair. She dusted a light film of powder over her shiny nose and tear-puffed eyes, and reluctantly left to keep her appointment with Marvin.

He was already seated at a table sipping coffee when Wendy arrived. She ordered orange juice, toast, and coffee, wondering if she would be able to eat. She recalled Sumnieng's words about tea tasting salty with unshed tears.

"I have the most wonderful news," Marvin began excitedly as soon as the waitress left the table. "The laboratory cabled me that the directors were very pleased with the progress I am making here, and have voted to name our new hybrid rice 'Mortimer's variety' in my honor."

"That's marvelous," said Wendy, trying to sound enthusiastic. She knew it really was an honor to have the new rice named after him, particularly since the new variety could make an important addition to the food supply in Asia.

Marvin outlined in detail all the contacts he had made and the promotions he had planned for Mortimer rice. Wendy sipped her coffee and nibbled her toast in a dispirited, preoccupied way.

"I don't think you've heard a word I've said," he accused when, during a pause, she failed to give the approving response he expected.

On the contrary, he hasn't given a single thought to me, hasn't really looked at me or sensed that something is wrong, she realized. How could he be so insensitive, so unaware of her distress, so oblivious to anyone's needs and feelings but his own? How unlike Erick, who had been so sensitive, so completely in tune with her moods and feelings.

She could see now that it had been the same with their non-wedding. Marvin had not given any thought to the feelings, cost, or embarrassment of her family or her when he saw an opportunity for his own advancement. In the same self-centered way, his attitude toward the Thai people, who would grow his rice, was one of condescension and insensitivity.

"Oh, yes, I've heard every word you said about Mortimer rice. I'm sure you'll do great things with it," she replied dutifully.

Mollified, Marvin started to launch into more detail, when he was interrupted by the arrival of a bellboy.

"Telephone for you, Miss Devin. You can take it in the lobby," he told her in a low voice.

She jumped up so suddenly that her purse clattered to the floor, but fortunately the contents did not spill. She scooped it up, and, restraining the urge to run, walked rapidly across the dining room and lobby to the indicated phone.

"Hello, this is Wendy," she identified herself anxiously.

"Wendy, this is Jane Adams," said a hesitant, throaty voice. "Have you seen the paper about Erick and the boy?"

"Yes," answered Wendy so low it was hardly audible.

"The planes went out last night as soon as he failed to report, and the helicopters went out as soon as it was light this morning. I thought the waiting might be easier for you out here where the search is being directed and where the first reports will come in. I'll be in the Hospital Staff lounge behind the main desk. Would you like to join me?"

Wendy murmured her thanks, and dashed across the lobby and out the main entrance where a line of taxis waited. She climbed into the first one and directed the driver, "Baansum Long Service Hospital, and please hurry."

Wendy was grateful that she had found a driver who spoke English. The taxi crept through Bangkok's morning traffic with agonizing slowness—beyond the modern buildings to the colorful, cluttered shops and crowded apartment houses, across *klongs* with their boats and stilt-supported shanties, and finally through lush fields of rice.

Rice! Marvin! She had dashed out after the phone call, leaving him sitting in the dining room, awaiting her return. She laughed helplessly and felt a little better. Waiting in a coffee shop wasn't like waiting at the altar, but it helped to balance the scales a little bit.

As the taxi turned into the curving drive of Baansum Hospital, Wendy realized that in her mad dash to get here nothing had been said about price.

"How much do I owe you?" she asked, forcing a smile.

The driver looked at the worried, drawn face of his passenger, shrugged, and replied, "Twenty baht."

Knowing that this was considerably less than the best price she could have bargained for, Wendy ignored the non-tipping tradition of the Thais and added ten baht to the price named. She walked rapidly through the coldly antiseptic reception room of the American service hospital, hesitating at the reception desk. Several people were waiting for the attention of the busy corpsman, so she turned down the hall. The second door on the right bore the inscription "Staff Lounge No Admittance." She knocked and was relieved when Jane, looking tense and tired, opened the door.

Wendy's apprehension rose when she entered the room and found Paul huddled at the table, listlessly sipping a cup of coffee. He was wearing flight gear.

"Can I get you a cup of coffee?" he greeted.

"Yes, please," she answered, knowing they were both postponing facing an unpleasant reality. "Have they learned anything about Erick?" she asked when he returned with a steaming mug of coffee.

"We lost radio contact last night right after he reported he was taking off with the boy," said Paul as if reciting an official report. "When he didn't arrive in the normal flying time and our radar monitor couldn't pick him up, it was too near dark for our choppers to fly to Chiengmai. Search and Rescue sent out jets, but they fly rather high and fast to spot anything on the ground. Our men have been searching the area since dawn."

Just then the Major came in.

"Any word?" asked Jane anxiously.

"Nothing yet. That's awfully rugged country. The helicopters are coming in to refuel." Turning to Paul he asked, "You going out this time?"

"I sure am."

"Search the bottoms of those valleys, but if you happen across any poppy fields, watch out for sniper fire."

"I know. If we happen to fly over a hidden opium field, they think we were sent to spy on them, and you never know what kind of arms those growers have."

Wendy drew in her breath sharply and the Major turned to look at her, as if he had been unaware there was an outsider present.

"Did they learn anything at all?" asked Jane doggedly.

She's in love with Erick too, thought Wendy, anguish and fear forcing her to face the depth of her own love for him.

"One of the copters carrying an interpreter landed on the logging camp air strip. They said Erick didn't seem to be having any trouble when he picked up the boy and took off, but we knew that from his radio contact. They're working on the north slope of the mountain so the helicopter would be out of sight as soon as it broke over the ridge. They have ground teams out searching. The boy belongs to an important family, so they're doing all they can, but there's heavy underbrush and it's hard going."

"I'll let you know if I spot anything," said Paul, moving rapidly to the door as a helicopter whirred overhead. The Major followed close behind, leaving the two girls staring anxiously after them.

Wendy looked at the trim, efficient nurse beside her and wondered how many people she had waited with while matters of life and death were decided. This time Wendy knew she shared the anxiety. Finally she voiced the thought that had haunted her since she had received Jane's call. "Was it like this when Jimmy Thompson went down?"

"We knew he'd been hit. He had radio contact and was able to give his position before he crashed. Erick and Tom were at the wreck within an hour," Jane answered, as if Wendy had almost read her thoughts.

"It must have been awful for them."

"Yes, I think that's when Tom decided to quit the squadron. He and Migin were engaged. You've met them?"

"I met them in Tahiti," Wendy answered. "They're delightful, and I loved their resort."

"I thought for a while Erick might join them. They wanted him to, but something brought him back to Bangkok."

Was Jane that something? Wendy wondered.

A helicopter sounded above them and the two girls moved to the window with one accord. As the helicopter reached the horizon, it was followed by five others across the sky like a string of awkward toys trailed by a child.

Time dragged slowly. "Have you been in Bangkok long?" Wendy asked when the waiting became unbearable.

"Almost five years. I was with the squadron when we first opened this Air-Evac operation. So were Erick, Tom, Jimmy Thompson, the Major, and Mike O'Connor."

"I met Mike in Bali. He's a real charmer," said Wendy.

"Yes, I almost married him three years ago," answered Jane matter-of-factly.

"What happened?" Wendy asked, regretting the words the moment they were out.

"When Jimmy was killed, Mike decided he couldn't ask a woman to share the hazards and uncertainties of this life. When his commitment was up, he went to Bali to start his own business. He said he would come back for me when he got it going. I didn't agree. When I marry I expect to share whatever risks my man's way of life involves him in, whether they are financial or personal."

Wendy thought with a pang how closely Jane and Erick worked together, sharing whatever danger or hardships their trips involved. Now she and Jane were sharing the endless waiting.

The Major came striding back into the room. "I think waiting is the hardest part," he said giving words to their thoughts. He was just finishing the cup of coffee Jane brought him when the phone rang. "Major Sims here," he answered. "Still nothing . . . an elephant you say—strange, but I guess there are lots of them up there. Tell the crews to keep looking."

His voice was strained as he turned to Jane. "They haven't found a thing—no sign of the helicopter or wreckage. Paul says there isn't a farm or a poppy field or anything else growing there except trees."

"What was that about an elephant?" Jane asked.

"Paul said the only living thing he saw was an elephant tramping around in a circle on a virtual rampage."

"There aren't any wild elephants up there," said Jane frowning. "Only those which have been brought in or raised there to help work the teak."

"That's right. One must have escaped from the logging camp."

"I didn't think the ones raised to work ever run away," said Wendy.

"They don't usually unless something happens to their mahout," replied the Major.

"Was the boy who was hurt an elephant boy?" asked Wendy.

"I don't know. Who handled the call, Jane?"

"The Emergency Room, I think. I'll get the record."

Jane returned in minutes and thrust the message in the Major's hands:

ELEPHANT PULLED TREE ON BOY—
CRUSHED LEG—REQUEST ASSISTANCE

"Sounds like an inexperienced elephant and an inexperienced boy. They might go together, but I'm not sure I see the connection," said the Major.

"Erick tells me that when a boy is given an elephant to raise, the elephant will follow the boy around like a big dog," Wendy said. "But you're right, I don't see how that could have anything to do with a helicopter. Guess I'm grasping at straws."

"We don't seem to have anything else to grasp at. Let's go over to the control room."

A young airman looked up from the radar scope on which he was concentrating and smiled appreciatively at his unexpected, attractive guests.

"Get me Captain Hess in the lead helicopter," barked the Major. In seconds Paul's voice was responding to the call. "Get back to where you saw the elephant. Go in as low as possible. Let me know if you see anything unusual at all," ordered the Major.

The airman indicated a bright blip on the radar screen, which suddenly reversed its direction and moved back along the path of the sweep. It stopped moving and Paul's voice came crackling back, tinged with excitement. "There's something there! It's back in the trees so I can't see what—might be another elephant—but something broke through the trees recently. There's no place to land, and I'm not sure I could get in anyway. That's one mad elephant."

"Just hover. I'll be right up with a pocketful of peanuts," answered the Major, the bounce returning to his voice. He turned to the excited spectators. "Anyone know where there's an experienced elephant handler?"

"There are some mahouts working their elephants at Timland. I saw them yesterday," answered Wendy.

The Major picked up the phone and dialed rapidly. "Get me an elephant trainer, one from the Chiengmai area . . . call Timland . . . call the Minister of Health if you have to, he owes me a favor . . . I don't care what it takes, just get one! Promise the trainer a ride in a helicopter. I'll pick him up on the parking lot at Timland with the admin chopper in fifteen minutes."

Wendy remembered Erick's remark about the Major being good at twisting arms.

Turning to Jane he said, "If anyone asks what you're doing up here, tell them you're monitoring my flight; I asked for a nurse and an assistant."

Wendy was grateful that the Major had included her in the anxious vigil.

Obviously a man more accustomed to action than to waiting, the Major strode out of the room, firing instructions to the sergeant who had fallen in step beside him.

"Does the Major fly his own helicopter?" Wendy asked.

"Not much anymore, but he's one of the best," said Jane, pride in her voice.

Wendy and Jane watched the small helicopter, the type used in police and traffic patrol, rise rapidly from the runway and head north. As it disappeared from sight, the airman monitoring the radar screen indicated a small, bright blip. It was visible only briefly and then disappeared.

"He's landing at Timland," explained the young man.

In a few minutes, the blip reappeared in the spot from which it had vanished. "It'll take him over an hour to get up there. You girls might as well relax."

Wendy watched the bright spots at the top of the radar screen, crossing and recrossing like bright shuttlecocks weaving an intricate pattern. Only one remained stationary. From the bottom of the screen a brighter image headed toward the others at a seeming snail's pace. Wendy finally walked away from the screen to a tower window facing north. Erick is up there somewhere, she thought. But will they find him? Is he alive—is he injured?

"Remember, they're trained to locate downed pilots. Rescue is part of what they're here for," said Jane, joining Wendy at the window.

"Suppose I started the Major off on a wild goose chase. Suppose there's no connection between the elephant and Erick's helicopter?" Wendy asked.

"Don't worry about that," answered Jane. "When they're on a search mission, they follow every lead, no matter how unlikely. They expect most of them to be blanks. A search party may follow dozens of useless leads before getting the one that pays off."

With agonizing slowness the small, bright spot from

the bottom of the screen approached the stationary one at the top.

"Admin calling Search Leader . . . What's going on now?" The Major's voice crackling on the intercom broke the silence of the control tower.

"Search Leader . . . Craziest thing I ever saw," Paul replied. "The elephant looks like a rookie on patrol. He comes crashing out of the timber, walks to a corner of the clearing, raises his trunk as if trumpeting at me, then he turns and goes to the other corner and does the same thing, and finally goes back into the trees a couple of hundred feet from where he came out."

"I'm coming in range," said the Major. "Next time the elephant comes out, hover over him all along his path to keep him distracted. I'll drop in behind him and lower my passenger. It'll be a ladder descent, not a jump, so keep the elephant too occupied to turn around," directed the Major.

The girls watched as the smaller spot approached the larger one on the radar screen until they were barely discernible as two distinct objects.

"He's coming out," warned Paul.

"Wait until he raises his trunk, then lead him along his usual path at fairly close range . . . that's it. The mahout says he can handle him. When he gets the elephant under control, lower your evacuation team at the opposite end of the clearing. The trainer doesn't seem to be having any trouble with the elephant, but slip your people in as carefully as possible—don't rock the boat," directed the Major.

A maddening silence followed while Wendy and

Jane could only watch the two bright specks on the radar as the other bright dots on the screen rapidly joined them like a convention of fireflies. Wendy's heart was pounding in her ears so loudly she wondered if Jane could hear it, but Jane's face remained immobile.

"Evac team reports it's the chopper!" shouted Paul. "Wings and rotor chewed up, but the fuselage appears to be intact."

"They're alive!" The crackling and static that punctuated that joyous shout indicated it came directly from the walkie-talkie carried by the evacuation team on the ground.

Jane and Wendy dissolved into tears simultaneously. The puzzled airman looked at them and shook his head dubiously.

"The corpsman has a splint on the boy's leg, and he's sedated. Erick's injured—jammed a leg on the rudder when they crashed." Paul resumed relaying details supplied from the ground.

"Bring them in," said the Major. "I'm going home. I'm almost out of gas in this baby buggy, and I see you have plenty of help—in fact, it looks like the squadron is holding an airbone convention."

"Let's go back to the hospital," said Jane. "It'll take them over an hour to get in. All you ever do in this outfit is wait." The relief in her voice denied the complaint in her words.

Wendy knew there would be a great deal this efficient nurse would do to prepare for the arrival of the two patients, not just wait. Wendy envied her having some activity to fill the remaining eternity of waiting.

Finally Wendy heard the whir of a helicopter and followed Jane out the emergency entrance to the landing pad. She expected to see the small administration helicopter the Major was flying, but instead it was a large army "flying banana" painted white with a red cross on its side. Portable steps were rolled in place almost before the giant blade ceased turning. Corpsmen with stretchers bounded up them. Wendy clenched her fists, fighting back the urge to go dashing up the stairs in search of Erick.

A few minutes later the corpsmen reappeared, carrying a boy who looked pathetically small on the big army stretcher. His right leg was strapped to a retaining board. As the sun struck his eyes, he raised a thin hand to shade them, and smiled broadly. Jane, who had been standing beside Wendy, moved quickly to the boy's side, took his hand, and began talking to him in Thai. For the second time that day, Wendy could feel the tears welling up in her eyes.

As she turned her face away, she saw Erick's blond head appear in the copter door. Wendy dashed to the stairs, but Erick was already swinging himself down them, supporting his weight on the handrails as he balanced on his right leg. Wendy stopped, holding her breath as she watched him, so ruggedly handsome in his flying gear.

When he reached the runway, he scooped her up with one arm while maintaining his balance with the other. He leaned his weight against her in the rush of their eager embrace. His lips crushed hers, releasing a flood of joy to replace the agony of fear-filled waiting. Her hands caressed his beloved face, clung convulsively around his neck, aware of nothing except the ecstasy of his return to her.

Slowly, reluctantly, he raised his head. As she opened her eyes, Wendy flushed with embarrassment to see Paul and the crew standing on the steps they were blocking. A corpsman had arrived with a wheelchair and was waiting to help Erick. The Major came striding around the tail of the copter. She had been so oblivious to everything but the sensation of Erick's nearness, that she hadn't even heard the other helicopter land.

"I know you have a thing about animals, but what's with you and that elephant?" the Major demanded of Erick with a twinkle in his eye.

"Sorry, I can't claim him," Erick said. "He belongs to Kau, the boy we brought in. Came crashing through the timber about daybreak. I was afraid he would tear apart what was left of the helicopter after that downdraft slammed us into the timber. Kau had the Thai corpsman carry him to the door, and shouted commands. The elephant began marching around like he was in a circus ring. The corpsman said he ordered the elephant to stand guard."

"Wendy figured it might be something like that from what you told her about those boys and their elephants," said the Major, giving her an approving look. "How do you suppose the elephant ever found you?"

"I don't know. Kau told the elephant to stay when we first boarded the helicopter. Last I saw of him, he was standing by the runway in the logging camp with his trunk raised. You never know about an elephant—

whether he heard or sensed something when we went down, or was just trying to follow us, crossing the ridge where the helicopter disappeared from his sight." Erick turned from the Major to Wendy, whose hand he was still holding. "But it's good to know a woman who listens to what you say about elephants and other things, and remembers it," he finished by pressing her hand gently to his lips.

Jane came briskly out of the emergency door and crossed quickly to Erick. "Welcome home, oh Lord of the Jungle," she teased. She threw her arms around his neck and gave him a big kiss which Erick returned with marked enthusiasm.

It was not the kiss, but the look of complete understanding which passed between them which sent Wendy's spirits crashing back to earth. It struck her with a pang that she was the one to meet Erick on his return because Jane had gone to tend the wounded boy—that it was Jane who had sensed her need to be there in the first place. How could she compete with someone like that, she thought, remembering the love she had sensed in Jane when Erick was missing.

"There's a man in X-ray who insists on seeing you," said Jane, taking command of the wheelchair.

CHAPTER TWELVE

It was almost eleven o'clock when Wendy awoke. She glanced at her travel alarm and stretched luxuriously. She hadn't slept that late since she left San Francisco. It felt great to be alive, to know that Erick was alive. She dressed carefully in the blue dress that was Erick's favorite.

Seated in the coffee shop, Wendy remembered how little she had eaten the previous day, and ordered the special brunch. The papaya was rich, mellow, and golden ripe; small hotcakes floated in coconut syrup; the jasmine tea was sweet and fragrant—today there were no salty unshed tears.

Even her timing was perfect. By the time she arrived at the hospital they would have finished serving lunch.

Waiting at the taxi stand was the cab that had taken her to the hospital the previous day.

"Baansum Hospital," she directed.

"You should bargain for the fare," chided the driver. "When a passenger looks as happy as you do, sometimes I charge them double."

Sensing the game the driver wished to play to relieve the boredom of his job, Wendy climbed out of the taxi and asked, "How much to Baansum Hospital?"

"Forty baht," he replied.

"What do you think I am, a tourist who does not know Bangkok? Yesterday a driver took me there for twenty baht," she said with mock indignation.

"We have a fuel crisis, too," responded the driver. "Yesterday an American lady paid me thirty baht."

"Fair enough," answered Wendy climbing back into the cab. They both laughed.

"Your friend in the hospital is better?" the driver asked when the traffic had thinned and no longer required his complete attention.

"Much better, thank you."

"Did you read in the newspaper about the elephant boy in the American helicopter?" he asked.

"Yes, it is Captain Randall I am going to visit," she admitted, feeling herself flush with excitement.

"Then it is truly a day to be happy," said the driver, pulling up in front of the hospital.

"Pardon me if I don't stand," quipped Erick as he lay with his left leg in massive bandages and firmly immobilized.

Wendy ran to the bed and threw her arms around him. He pulled her to him and pressed his lips hungrily to hers. She clung to him as if the fates that had brought him back might snatch him away again. Her happiness, the tingling excitement which flooded through her, left no doubt that he was the man for her. She shuddered to think that she might have lost him. Tears began to squeeze out of the corners of her tightly closed eyes and form beads under her long lashes.

"Hey, I'm back. I'm all right," he said, lightly kissing her eyelids, her cheeks, her lips.

Wendy opened her eyes, feeling the tips of her long lashes brush against his cheek. She looked at him, hoarding every detail of his face and voice in her memory, knowing that whatever happened she would always love this man.

Even as she watched, his eyes changed, clouded as if a curtain had been dropped over them. There would be no further communication between them, no loving message like the one he had flashed to Jane yesterday when she came to meet him. This memory, which she had been blocking out all day, rose to taunt her. Slowly Wendy pulled back from the man whose lips promised love to one girl, while his eyes promised love to another.

"I hear you're quite the hero now," she said, imitating Erick's usual light and playful mood.

"The way I hear it, I'm getting second billing to an elephant," he replied, matching her teasing. "But the unsung heroine is you—the one who listened, remembered, and used that smart little head to figure out what was going on," he said, entwining his fingers in hers and looking at her with admiration.

"I'm afraid one good idea wouldn't have been worth much without the Major and Jane to put it into action," she answered blushing.

"The Major is quite a character," agreed Erick. "Yesterday he was doing what he does best, getting everyone's cooperation, organizing and leading an emergency mission. And our girl Jane seems to always be on hand when we need her."

She even understood how I needed to feel a part of the search and brought me into it, thought Wendy miserably.

"You should have seen the squadron when we first came to Thailand," he continued, warming to his subject. "All of us competing for Jane's attention."

"I can imagine," said Wendy, letting bitterness at the thought of losing him again triumph over her feeling of gratitude to Jane.

"I believe you're jealous of Jane," he said in a tone that suggested a deeper meaning to the teasing. This annoyed Wendy even more. The conceit of him, she thought, so sure I'm one of his conquests that he can taunt me about being jealous. But she was honest enough to admit to herself that he was right.

A light tapping on the door cut short any reply. It took Wendy a moment to recognize the saffron-robed monk standing in the doorway as Tahn. He raised a hand to his shaved head as if removing the familiar red cap and waving it in the air. Erick pressed his hands together and made as much of a *wai* as was possible lying flat on his back with one foot raised in the air.

This is truly Peter Pan and one of the boys who never grew up, thought Wendy, the anger of a moment before dissolving in their contagious good humor.

"I told my teacher that my uncle was in the hospital in Bangkok, and I must go and see him," said Tahn. "He said: 'The American uncle who gave you the beautiful book of *Jataka Tales?*' He says it is the most beautiful book he ever saw. He arranged for my leave to come visit you."

"You bring sunshine to match the color of your robes," said Erick in a tone Wendy had never heard before. The fleeting glimpses of unsuspected depths in him never ceased to amaze her.

The moment passed as suddenly as it had come.

"The monks of your monastery should have grown fat with such a pirate as you to collect the food," teased Erick.

"I thought yesterday you were going to bring us an elephant," replied Tahn, giving as good as he received. "Your leg, is it broken?" he asked, shifting to a tone of concern.

"No, just the . . . muscles," replied Erick searching for a word Tahn would understand. "I'll be back skiing by the time you are. How is your family?"

"They are well. There is very good news for my sister Kokay. After you and Miss Jane came to our house for my party, my family agreed to let Kokay come to school in Bangkok to study to be a nurse. Miss Jane arranged that she does not have to pay the school because she is a very good student."

"Oh, a scholarship," Erick added.

More of Jane's quiet, efficient caring, Wendy thought. She was also aware of the manner in which Tahn had linked Jane and Erick together in speaking of their visit. Everyone seemed to feel that they belonged together. She was happy for the shy, lovely Kokay, whom she had first noticed sitting in the corner making paper flowers for the temple. She hardly seemed the equal of emergency rooms and sickbeds, but there was an unsuspected strength behind the delicate beauty of Thai women. Wendy remembered how Kokay had come shyly forward to speak English with her, and to examine in fascination the tiny charms on her bracelet. When Wendy complimented her on the lovely flowers she was making, Kokay had replied, "They are not so beautiful as the tiny gold flower on your arm."

As Tahn and Erick resumed their playful banter, Wendy removed the small golden forget-me-not from her bracelet. In spite of Marvin's poetic note, Wendy knew now that the only way the scales of love could be balanced was to put an equal amount on both sides. Neither forgiveness alone nor a lovely gold forget-me-not could make up for a lack of love. She handed the little charm to Tahn and said, "Please give this to Kokay and wish her success for me."

Tahn examined the workmanship appreciatively, wrapped the charm in a tissue from Erick's bedside, and tucked it carefully in a leather pouch hanging on his belt. "I fear I must start back now. It is a long walk to the place where I catch the bus for my village, and I must not be late for evening prayers."

"If you will hail a cab and bargain with the driver for me, we can ride downtown together," said Wendy, remembering how Tahn had been waiting for her at the airport when she arrived in Bangkok.

"It is proper that I should walk," replied Tahn, "but it is also proper that I should help a stranger in our land, so I will help you find your way with the taxi."

"I'm so glad you're all right," Wendy told Erick, squeezing his hand. Was she using Tahn's presence as an excuse not to betray her feelings by kissing Erick again? she wondered.

He lifted her hand lightly to his lips, and let her go. To Tahn he said, "Please give my best wishes to your family, and my thanks to your teacher for allowing you to visit your American uncle."

"Will you take more ski lessons when I return from the monastery?" asked Tahn in the taxi.

"I'm afraid not. I have to go to Hong Kong, then back to San Francisco," Wendy answered.

"You don't like Bangkok?"

"Oh, yes, I like Bangkok very much, but it is my job to find places other people would like to visit and arrange tours for them. I must get back to my job."

"I'll bet Erick could find a job for you in Bangkok," said Tahn.

Wendy wished that were true, but the fact that she had no part in the job Erick and Jane shared seemed to be one of the problems keeping them apart.

"There is a temple near the place where I catch my bus that I will show you. I think your tourists would like to see Wat Trimitr, temple of the gold Buddha," said Tahn.

"I thought most images of Buddha were gold."

"No, most Buddhas are other material covered with thin gold. The Buddha at Wat Trimitr is gold all the way through. He is only ten feet tall, but weighs more than five tons. He is in a small, new temple downtown. This Buddha is special to me because he came out of hiding the year I was born. The crane putting the Buddha in the new temple dropped him and chipped the plaster which was used to hide the gold from raiders long ago. With my people it is not a great temple because it is not old and known to their ancestors, but Americans like to go there. They like to think about all that gold."

Wendy laughed in spite of herself at Tahn's shrewd typecasting of both Thais and Americans.

She could not see the temple from the main street where the taxi stopped, but Tahn led her to an entrance down a narrow sidestreet. He had been right about an American's reaction to the statue, Wendy thought as she caught her breath at the deep glowing beauty of the figure, smaller than most, sitting in the modest temple whose principal decorations were light, airy woodcarvings.

When she had fully enjoyed the lovely jewel of a temple and its priceless treasures, Wendy returned her attention to the slightly built monk in saffron robes standing beside her. Completely absorbed in his prayers, he too revealed another, deeper part of himself.

Wendy's farewell to Tahn left her depressed. His alternating happy and serious moods had caused her to relax, to forget for a while the pain of the realization that Jane was the woman with whom Erick would share his life.

Reluctant to return to the loneliness of her room, she found a seat in a secluded corner of the lobby where she could observe and listen to the comments of tourists beginning to return from afternoon tours. In the past their reactions had been helpful in organizing her own plans.

Since the publicity given the rescue of Erick and the boy as well as the part played in it by the elephant and the mahout, Timland had become a popular destination. The remarks Wendy heard were enthusiastic about the Thai crafts, dance and martial arts performances, and particularly about the elephants at work.

When most of the tourists had gone on to their rooms, Wendy noticed a middle-aged couple waiting nervously on the other side of the lobby. There was something vaguely familiar about the tall, gray-haired, scholarly looking man who stood watching the entrance expectantly. She must have seen him in a tour group somewhere, Wendy decided, although she did not have the same feeling of recognition for the slightly plump, matronly woman standing beside him.

From somewhere behind her came the cry, "Daaaddy!" and like an animated doll Urai came flying across the lobby.

The man Wendy had been watching scooped Urai up and tossed her in the air as Erick had done. As he lowered the giggling, shrieking child, he turned to the woman beside him who was shyly holding out her arms. He gently handed Urai to his wife, who lovingly gathered the little girl to her.

Turning her head, Wendy saw Paul and Sumnieng going toward the older couple. Suddenly Wendy realized that the man she had been watching seemed familiar because he looked like an older version of Paul. Already the big man was closing the distance between himself and Sumnieng—holding out his arms to her. Sumnieng's apprehensive expression turned to mixed embarrassment and pleasure as he gave her a big bear hug.

As the trio turned to Paul's mother, she continued to cuddle Urai as if defying anyone to take the child from her. Sumnieng's graceful *wai* caused a startled, confused look to cross the older woman's face. She solved the dilemma by freeing one arm from around Urai and slipping it around Sumnieng's shoulders while she kissed her cheek.

A feeling of shared happiness surged through Wendy, who for the second time had been an unintentional spectator at a very emotional meeting in Sumnieng's life. As before, she sat very still, lest her presence become an intrusion on the happiness of the small group across the room.

CHAPTER THIRTEEN

Again Wendy slept fitfully, but this time it was Jane who cavorted through her dreams, prancing and jabbing with the giant paper vaccination needle as she had at Tahn's party. Waking slowly, Wendy giggled at the image which her dreams had produced. At least laughing at herself was a good sign, she thought as she slipped reluctantly out of bed, determined to do what she knew had to be done.

After breakfast she stopped at the Thai Airways reservation desk in the lobby and made her reservation for Hong Kong on the following morning's flight. She began making a list of the things she wanted to do on this, her last day in Bangkok. First she would go to the hospital and say good-bye to Erick. This time she would take a note from the comedians—or was it Erick himself whose philosophy was always leave them laughing. She would not let anyone worry about breaking her heart.

Wendy waited until almost ten o'clock, when Bangkok's morning traffic had thinned, before taking a cab to Baansum Long Service Hospital for the third consecutive day. When she paused to knock on Erick's partially open door, she was startled to see that he was gone.

"Has Captain Randall been moved?" Wendy asked the young Thai nurse busily filling out records behind the desk.

"Captain Randall left about an hour ago with Miss Jane."

"I didn't expect him to be released so soon."

"He was not released, just signed out on leave. When Miss Jane came in so happy and excited, they talk. Then she gets crutches for him and they go out."

"You said he signed out. When is he due back?" Wendy asked.

"Tonight at ten o'clock when the hospital closes."

Gone for the whole day! Wendy was stunned by this unexpected turn of events. She couldn't leave Bangkok without telling Erick good-bye. Never to see Erick again—the thought was unbearable. Slowly she realized that never seeing him again was exactly what she faced, with or without the brief parting she had planned. She could, of course, change her reservations for Hong Kong to the following day, but she wasn't sure she could bear to come back to the hospital again. She never had liked hospitals and was beginning to hate the place. Perhaps he wouldn't even be here tomorrow. She could hardly call and make an appointment. Wendy pictured Jane and Erick leaving together, laughing and joking in spite of his crutches.

As she thought of Jane, so poised, so in command of any situation, Wendy wondered what had happened to excite her so much that even the Thai nurse was aware of it. Had she and Erick resolved whatever differences had kept them apart? The relationship and the problem obviously went back long before Wendy had met Erick. She couldn't even claim the role of other woman in their triangle. Certainly there had been no animosity between them that fateful day when Erick was missing. Had the crisis resolved their problem? Had Erick asked Jane to marry him? Perhaps by not seeing Erick, she had been spared the role of cheerful loser—it was not a role she played very well.

The ride back to town was hot and oppressive. Only the long list of things which must be done on her last day in Bangkok kept her from retreating to the air-conditioned comfort of her room. First she must buy the deep-blue star sapphire pendant she had promised herself—that should raise her spirits if anything could.

The pendant was lovely. A perfect star twinkled brightly from the center of the brilliant blue stone—the color of Erick's eyes, she had told herself when she first saw it. Now she amended the comparison to the color of the lagoon in Moeréa—but that was no better. Would the stone forever remind her of Erick, she wondered as she hesitated over buying it. Did she want a reminder of the happy days they had spent together, or was it best just to try to forget? It was too soon to know; the hurt was too fresh.

Seeing her hesitation, the owner draped the pendant over his hand and held it closer for her to admire. "Notice how perfectly the star is centered," he said. "There is a legend that if one wears the stone of the magic star which is perfect and true, his love will also be true."

Wendy had heard of star-crossed lovers, but this was a new approach, a star to ward off such tragedy. The star in the jewel winked invitingly. It was as perfect a stone as she had seen, so, after proper negotiations over price, she bought it. She started to put the small box in her purse.

"Oh, no, miss, you must wear it so the star can reply to the pulse which beats in your throat." Apparently he believed his own legend, Wendy thought. She took the pendant out of the box and put it around her neck, carefully fastening the safety clasp. The merchant held up a mirror for her inspection. The sparkling blue sapphire looked lovely against her bronzed skin, and the star hung perfectly true. It would take more than a small silver star to bring back her true love, but she did feel better.

Next she must buy the piece of carved teakwood for her mother. She wanted to buy this directly from the artist who made it, so she took a taxi to Phra Mane Park. This was the first Saturday she had been free to attend the weekend market held there. She found herself among a noisy confusion of portable stalls covered by cloth awnings, which were erected each market day by farmers, craftsmen, and small merchants. The same array of fruit and vegetables she had seen at the floating market was offered here. She skirted gingerly around the most odorous of the fish stalls, and did not find the hanging poultry inviting either. The standard items of Thai dress—white shirts and blouses, dark trousers and long wrap skirts such as Sumnieng wore on her visit—were amply offered, as were underwear and shoes. Bolts of material were artfully draped to suggest their appearance in the finished product. She wished she could bring her mother some of the beautiful native plants. A wide variety of small, delicate orchids, some of which she had never seen before, were displayed against plants with bold, vivid tropical foliage. She knew that these plants were strictly forbidden by the plant quarantine, so she turned her attention to the cluster of stalls offering carved teakwood. She examined one beautifully carved piece after another, pausing to watch artists whose skilled hands were busy with new creations. Finally she found the figure of a Thai dancer for whose classically beautiful face Sumnieng might have been the model. It was a gift for her mother, but Wendy knew it would give her pleasure whenever she saw it.

She left the park on the side adjoining the Grand Palace, and paused for a moment to enjoy the panoramic view of brilliant, multi-tiered, red-and-gold roofs spiked with graceful spires above gleaming white walls. She would have liked to enjoy a last look at the exquisite Emerald Buddha, but time was growing short and the business part of her last day in Bangkok was not complete.

She took a taxi back to the modern, bustling, downtown section of the city and spent the balance of the afternoon at the office of Personal World Tour's Bangkok representative. She checked carefully the details of the tours she had been working on. There was so much to be worked out for the "People to People" program she planned to present to Mr. Vance. She hoped to arrange invitations for small groups to visit private homes, hobby and special interest groups, and small village functions. There would have to be cars instead of buses for transportation, and interpreters available where needed, although she had found English spoken quite widely in Thailand.

When the office closed at six, she walked to the corner where she noticed again the small spirit house in front of the Visitor's Bureau. Erick had said that people working for the tourist bureau brought offerings. Since tours of Thailand were to be her specialty, it seemed only fitting to do her part. She placed a lighted candle in the dollhouse-sized shrine.

There was just one item remaining on her list. She took a taxi to the Dusit Thani to leave a note for Marvin. She couldn't leave without a word, even though he deserved none. He was a person of such regular habit, she knew he would be at dinner and that there was no risk of running into him.

Wendy had a little trouble convincing the clerk to put her brief note in Marvin's box. Since Marvin was in the hotel, he couldn't understand why she didn't deliver the message in person. She finally persuaded him that Marvin would be in the dining room and that she didn't want to disturb him. The clerk looked at her dubiously, as if he doubted that such a pretty girl would be a disturbance or that anyone would be having dinner as early as six o'clock. The traditional dinner hour in Thailand, as in most warm countries, is much later. But he smiled slyly and put the note in the appropriate pigeon hole.

Wendy turned instinctively toward the express elevator to the observation tower but, remembering it adjoined the dining room, changed her mind. She just wasn't up to an encounter with Marvin.

Her mission accomplished, Wendy stopped on the steps to feed peanuts to the hotel's baby elephant—a thank-you for the help an elephant had given in finding Erick.

"Any friend of Tiny is a friend of mine," said a hopeful American voice behind her.

Wendy was in no mood to become involved with a lonely American looking for a friendly face from home. With a deliberately aloof look she turned to confront a tall, grinning, red-haired man.

"Mike O'Connor!"

"The little green-eyed leprechaun," he said, holding out a large hand which completely engulfed hers.

"What are you doing in Bangkok?"

"Trying to be a knight on a white horse, I guess—but as usual my timing was off."

"I seem to be having the same problem," she replied with more bitterness than she had intended.

"How about drowning our sorrows together?" When she seemed about to refuse, he hurried on. "Or dinner? I have a friend who dances at one of the Thai restaurants. I really would like to see her before I go back to Bali."

"Sumnieng?"

"Oh, you've met Sumnieng. How is she?"

"She is being acclaimed one of the most talented dancers in Bangkok—so beautiful, such a marvelous person," said Wendy with enthusiasm. "I would like to see her dance again before I leave, but we'd be lucky to get a table on such short notice."

"So you're leaving too. When?"

"Tomorrow morning."

"Then it's agreed, we will say our farewells to Bangkok tonight at the Baan Thong. Don't worry about the reservation—I have a friend."

"You sound like the Major."

"So you've met the whole crew—I should have known."

Changing the subject, Wendy asked, "Can we stop by the Siam so I can freshen up? It's been a long day."

"Meet me in the bar," he said when they arrived at her hotel, "and if you take longer than two drinks' time, you could be sorry you accepted the invitation."

Although she didn't take Mike's warning too seriously, Wendy showered and dressed quickly. Selecting the right clothes was no problem—a green dress for Mike, one with a full skirt for sitting on the floor cushions of the Baan Thong. She noted the contrast between the blue sapphire twinkling at her throat and the green dress, and replaced the pendant with carved jade beads.

When Wendy entered the cocktail lounge, Mike was staring morosely into a half-empty glass. "Better have one while I finish this," he said, patting the stool beside him.

Wendy ordered the banana liqueur that is a specialty of Thailand.

"I thought that was for after dinner," he teased, his mood brightening.

"Among the sophisticated I suppose it is, but it smells so good, tastes sweet and cool, and I like the way it shimmers crystal clear over ice. It'll drown sorrows as well as the whiskey you're drinking."

"An Irish lass who scorns good whiskey," replied Mike in a deep brogue.

"I still have one friend who hasn't forgotten me. We have our dinner reservations," he said as he tossed down the rest of the whiskey and waited for Wendy to finish sipping her drink.

Wendy felt memories begin to nag at her as they crossed the bridge and entered the Baan Thong restaurant where she had first met Jane, the Major, and Paul.

"So I'm not your one true love," complained Mike with mock injury when they had been seated at a front-row table and given their order. "You took off the sapphire with the perfect star," he explained in answer to Wendy's puzzled look.

Involuntarily her hand went to her throat and she blushed with confusion.

"I bought one like that for a girl once—lot of good it did," he complained.

"Jane?"

He nodded miserably.

"Is she why you are here?"

Again he nodded. "When I heard on the radio that Erick was lost, I pictured Jane all alone, feeling abandoned—a repeat of all the bad times after Jimmy was killed—so I caught the first flight for Bangkok. But there was a tropical storm and I didn't arrive until this morning."

"And by that time Erick had been rescued," prompted Wendy.

"Not only that, but when I got to the hospital to see Jane, they told me she was gone for the day with one of her patients. I thought I'd drop in to see Erick and congratulate him, but he was gone too. That age-old story, best pal and best gal." He stopped abruptly as he saw the pained look on Wendy's face. "Guess you don't need me adding my troubles to your own."

"That's all right. I already knew the story. I was there too, must have just missed you," she said, grateful for the concern in his eyes. Even in his own misery he was not insensitive to her unhappiness.

"I must be out of my mind mooning about another girl when I'm having dinner with the prettiest colleen outside of the Emerald Isle."

"Thanks, Mike, my ego needed that," said Wendy, her green eyes recapturing some of their usual sparkle.

"In romantic geometry, does that make us a square or a double triangle?" he asked.

Wendy smiled. If misery loved company, she certainly had some of the best.

Attractively arranged Thai dishes began to arrive. The beautiful girls in silk sarongs dropped effortlessly to their knees in spite of the huge trays they carried, and arranged the dishes on the low teak table. Determined not to act like a schoolgirl who demonstrates her heartbreak by nibbling at her food, Wendy attacked the delicious morsels with enthusiasm.

"The condemned man ate a hearty meal," quipped Mike as he demolished a dish of crisped duck sprinkled with ground peanuts.

As they finished the last bite of fresh melon, the houselights dimmed and the entertainment began. As before, the polite applause which marked the end of the opening number swelled to an ovation as Sumnieng appeared. Wendy sat entranced as she watched the beautiful girl perform the ancient rituals.

"Whew! She is something," enthused Mike when the number was completed. "Guess I have spent my share of time watching temple dancers and others throughout the Orient, but I have never seen anyone to match her beauty and grace."

"Who is the Stagedoor Johnny at the front table? His eyes followed Sumnieng like he'd seen every performance she ever gave," said Mike when Sumnieng had concluded her final number and the applause had died down.

"You didn't know Paul Hess?" Wendy asked with surprise. "I guess he joined the squadron after you left. I think you are right about his seeing every performance when he's not flying. Those are his parents sitting with him, just arrived yesterday to meet Sumnieng. From what I saw, they may not let Paul come home if he doesn't bring Sumnieng and Urai with him."

"I'm glad; she deserves some happiness," said Mike. "Have you seen Urai? She was the cutest baby I ever saw."

"She is a perfect little doll, a miniature of her

mother. She has an absolute hangup on American daddies. I guess she has had a full squadron of them."

"Wish I could see her and Sumnieng too, but I have reservations on the early-morning flight to Bali. They haven't changed the rules about going backstage, have they?"

"Afraid not. Sounds like you are an old-timer here."

"Jane and I used to . . ." replied Mike but his voice trailed off.

"Sorry," said Wendy, the moments of forgetfulness shattered by their mutual memories.

"The perfect dramatic conclusion for our soap opera tragedy," said Mike when the rain began to come down in sheets as they waited under the covered portico for a taxi.

Streetlights became dim blurs through the deluge of water. In a matter of minutes the street was running full of water from curb to curb. All traffic stopped and people huddled under whatever shelter they could find. With almost unbearable longing, Wendy recalled the tropical storm on Mooréa when she and Erick had huddled in a cave behind a rock.

"Hey, are you cold?" asked Mike, slipping a protective arm around her shoulders as he noticed her shiver. "It won't be this bad for long."

Wendy wasn't sure whether he meant the rain or the misery that they shared.

CHAPTER FOURTEEN

Wendy quickly completed the packing which she had neglected for her dinner with Mike the previous evening. She made a final check of the room and picked up the twinkling star sapphire pendant from her dressing table, where she had laid it the night before. She started to put it in her purse but, realizing that wearing a valuable piece of jewelry is safer than carrying it in a purse or suitcase, she put it on. Glancing at her watch, she saw that there were still two hours before she needed to leave for the airport. The rain-washed freshness of the day looked so inviting from the window of her room that she decided to take a walk.

As she stepped out onto the lawn surrounding the hotel, the fresh morning air was filled with the chattering of monkeys and the calls of myna birds from the garden. "Erick says you will like the garden,"

Tahn had told her the day she arrived. She crossed the rain-swollen *klong* and entered the beckoning garden. The honey-colored monkeys, who considered it their duty to inspect all visitors, frolicked along the path in front of her. Brilliant pink and turquoise cockatoos darted from the trees. The delicate petals of night blooming cereuses were gently closing, their life cycle spent. A sweet, spicy fragrance filled the air, and she followed the scent to the base of a tall tree from whose branches spilled a cascade of purple orchids. She hadn't realized that orchids smelled so sweet in their native state. As she watched, a small black form scooted up the tree and broke off one of the blooms, placed it in his teeth like a pirate's dagger, and came scooting back down. The white-ruffed monkey Erick called the General presented the orchid to Wendy with all the solemnity of a prom date. Just as seriously, she rewarded him with the peanuts which had spilled into her purse from the bag she had given the baby elephant. "Thank you for the bon voyage," she told him, tucking the orchid in her hair Tahitian fashion.

In the tranquility of the classic Siamese garden, loneliness enveloped her again. She felt as if her first day in Bangkok were a film running in reverse. She smiled crookedly as she imagined herself being pulled backward up the stairs of the plane and into her seat, then the plane flying backward to Tahiti—back to the bliss of those first carefree days with Erick. As she came around the corner by the lotus pond where he had been waiting that first day, the imaginary film broke; other lovers locked in embrace stood in their place. Was she destined always to be a spectator to someone else's love? Tears welling up in her eyes, she turned her head away, but in that instant she recognized that the trim blonde eagerly kissing the tall man who held her was Jane! But the man who held her close was not Erick—it was Mike! In confusion, Wendy tried to retreat behind a tall Croton, but in spite of Mike's preoccupation, he had seen her.

"You're too late, little leprechaun. I've already found the pot of gold at the end of the rainbow," he said with a wide grin spreading across his handsome Irish face.

"Wendy, we were looking for you," added Jane, flushed with happiness and looking less composed, less professional than Wendy had ever seen her.

"We couldn't let you go without letting you know how well the charm of a perfect sapphire star works, even if they are sometimes awfully slow," Mike continued.

"What happened?" Wendy asked, trying to conceal her surprise at the turn of events.

"We were all in the staff lounge talking about the plans for the Kau Clinic to be built on the timber reserve. Kau is the boy Erick rescued," explained Jane. "His father is a foreman with the teak company, and he and other company officials were so pleased with the rescue and the stories about the boy and his elephant that the company is establishing the clinic in Kau's honor. Erick and the Major were invited to the ceremonies at the Ministry of Health yesterday when the grant was presented. I'll be in charge of training the nurses," said Jane with professional pride.

"That's where everyone was yesterday when we went calling," added Mike with a wink.

"What a boost for your work," said Wendy, still wondering what it all had to do with reuniting Jane and Mike.

"While we were still talking about it," continued Jane, "Paul came in to tell us about his engagement to Sumnieng. He casually mentioned seeing you at the Baan Thong with a big red-headed American who Sumnieng said was an old friend of mine. I may not be Irish, but I really exploded." Jane looked searchingly from Wendy to Mike to be sure her earlier suspicions were not true. "I haven't worked such a miserable shift since I joined the army."

"Woman must work, and man must wait," said Mike, still grinning.

"You're going to stay here?" Wendy asked surprised.

"If I can find a razor and clean shirt big enough to fit me. My luggage is on its way back to Bali."

"Did you miss the plane?"

"I was in line to board when this wench come running up, threw her arms around me, and said, 'please don't go.' What could a frustrated knight in shining armor do?"

"He picked me up and carried me out of the terminal with all those people looking at us and smiling," said Jane, as embarrassed as a schoolgirl. "To think it took me two years to find the three magic words 'please don't go.'"

"You never seemed to need me before," said Mike. "When I heard Erick was missing, I thought you might, so I came flying back to Bangkok, and almost blew it again in a fit of jealousy." He kept one arm around her protectively as he spoke.

"We're being married tomorrow. Can't you stay over for the wedding?" asked Jane with a radiance which foretold what a beautiful bride she would be.

"I-I can't," stammered Wendy. "I have a business appointment in Hong Kong I wouldn't be able to postpone," she lied, not too convincingly. The thought of a wedding no longer upset her, but Erick would be there and she just couldn't bear to watch him valiantly trying to hide the hurt of losing Jane to Mike. She wanted no part of holding the hand of a man on the rebound. She had learned her lesson about love based on less than total commitment.

With a look of quick understanding, Mike said, "Then let us take you to the airport."

"If you showed up there again with two women, that would really confuse things," said Wendy, trying desperately for a light touch. "Thanks, but the airport limo is picking me up in ten minutes." She kissed Jane's cheek and held out her hand to Mike, who squeezed it gently. Then she turned and resolutely walked away. Her pace became more and more rapid as the shrubbery hid her from the happy lovers. As the contrast of her own hopeless love crushed in on her, she ran blindly up the path toward the *klong*.

"Not so fast, I'm flying on one wing," called the familiar voice she thought she might never hear again.

Flying wasn't a bad description, Wendy thought as she turned to see Erick coming toward her with surprising speed and agility, in spite of his crutches. She longed to rush into his arms and hold him in a close embrace that would need no crutches for support. They had not needed them the magic moment when he limped down the steps of the rescue helicopter and caught her in his arms—but that was before she had seen the look that told her he was in love with Jane. In a torment of conflicting emotions, she waited.

His headlong rush toward her stopped just as hers had done, as if halted by an invisible barrier.

"What are you doing here?" she asked in a reasonably steady voice.

"Playing hookey," he answered, pausing to catch his breath. "When I called, the switchboard operator said you had checked out."

"How did you know where to find me?"

"Chai was at the desk when I arrived. He said you hadn't left yet. I hoped you would come to the garden to say good-bye to the General and his friends on such a beautiful morning." He shifted his position awkwardly. "I've got to get off these damn things." He dropped smoothly to a stone bench beneath a plumeria tree and, taking her hand gently, pulled her down beside him.

"You were right about the General, he picked this farewell gift," she said, indicating the orchid in her hair.

"I wondered who my new competition was. He is a very smart monkey—that's how he got to be General. But I can't let him get ahead of me," he said, pulling a small box from his pocket. The box contained a tiny gold elephant, its trunk raised as if trumpeting.

"Oh, Erick, he's beautiful!" she said, throwing her

arms around his neck and kissing him lightly on the cheek.

He let the opportunity she offered pass. "A replacement for the forget-me-not you gave Kokay. Elephants are for remembering too."

"How could I forget the elephants of Thailand when one helped locate you?" She was struggling vainly to keep her voice light and not betray the deep longing she felt. "How did you know the flower I gave Kokay was a forget-me-not?"

"I noticed it when you added it to your charm bracelet the night after we first met in Tahiti. I knew it meant someone back home was waiting for you—not an encouraging sign."

"You certainly are observant."

"I try not to miss a detail where you're concerned," he said. Then, watching her face closely, he asked, "Was it from the man who just came to Bangkok, Marvin Mortimer?"

She smiled inwardly, pleased that he had been concerned enough about his competition to find out the name. She nodded. "We were to have been married."

"It's over?"

"It was a mistake from the start." She handed the little gold elephant back to him and indicated the empty place on her bracelet. "Please put it on."

"I see it's not the only new remembrance," he said as he finished attaching the charm to her bracelet and raised his hand to touch the gleaming star of the pendant at her throat. "From Mike?" he asked.

"How did you know I've seen Mike?"

"I was in the hospital staff room when Paul came in to announce his engagement to Sumnieng, and mentioned seeing you at the Baan Thong with Mike. I don't think I have ever seen Jane so upset. I have seen her in all kinds of emergencies in the last five years, but it was the first time I have ever seen her cry."

"What did she do?"

"She was on duty last night. She straightened everything her hands touched, ran needless errands, paced, and moped. When she went off duty I persuaded her to call the Dusit Thani where he always stayed, but when she called, he had already left for the airport. I reminded her that check-in time is two hours ahead of departure on international flights. She must have made it. I just passed them on the path." He chuckled, a deep throaty sound that sent a shiver through her.

"I thought Jane was in love with you, she seemed so distressed when you were missing. She sure acted like a woman waiting for the man she loves."

"She was waiting to see if I could keep my promise again," he said quietly.

"Your promise?"

"When our first assignments were up after Jimmy Thompson was killed, each of us—Tom, Mike, and I—went off to work out the shock and pain in our own way, leaving the Major and Jane with a couple of raw replacements to carry on the work of the squadron. Paul was one of them. Jane was discouraged and desperate when I got back from Tom's wedding. I told her then that I agreed our work was more important than anything else in the world, and I could always be counted on to come back and help."

"So Jane *was* the girl in Bangkok Migin told me you came back for?"

"How you women do talk. Yes, it was Jane, but not for the reason Migin and Niki assumed. She was also why it was so important for me to get released from that assignment to the Pentagon. What a reunion it was. You should have seen the look of triumph Jane gave me when I made it back with the boy."

"I did. That's when I knew you were in love with her."

"In love with Jane? You mistook admiration and mutual interest for love. So did I at first. When we all came to Bangkok, I was one of the pack of Jane's eager suitors. Then I realized it was all a matter of ego, competing to be the choice of the most popular girl in the crowd. Once I realized that, I began to grow up— to find real meaning in my work and my relationships with people, both men and women, American and Thai. Sumnieng and Jimmy helped me learn the real meaning of love."

How could he be so understanding, so able to communicate with everyone but her, she wondered.

He turned his head away a moment, then continued. "I've known I was in love with you since that day on Mooréa when the flash flood almost snatched you away from me. When I came down the steps and found you waiting after the helicopter rescue, I hoped for one wild moment that I could have it both ways— do the work that is my way of life, and come home to find you waiting. But when I saw the tears in your beautiful green eyes at the hospital, I knew I couldn't risk bringing you sorrow, asking you to endure the waiting and anguish this life might bring you."

"What kind of china doll do you think I am?" she demanded, her green eyes blazing and the charms on her bracelet jangling as she pulled free of the arm encircling her. "Do you think Jane is the only woman with the courage and self-reliance to share a life of danger and uncertainty?"

"When your Irish temper explodes, you're like a kitten with its back arched," he said, stroking her hair and silencing her outburst with a kiss.

It would be so easy to return his kiss, to nestle in his arms and leave the big questions of their lives unsettled while he played the role of noble protector. Defying every instinct of her surging emotions, Wendy pulled away from his embrace, determined to face the issue.

"I've seen you stand up to whatever came your way, from tropic storms to missing helicopters, and that's part of the girl I love. But because I love you, I want to make you happy, not someday bring you sorrow." He pressed his lips to her throat at the V formed by the star-sapphire pendant.

Trembling with desire, she pressed his head to her and stroked his temples. Her pulse pounded in her throat beneath the pendant, just as the legend had foretold. But the legend had only promised that her love would be true, not that they would find happiness together. Mike had said: "Sometimes the magic works awfully slow," but she couldn't risk the waiting.

Softly she said, "Mike says being needed and

wanted makes everything else unimportant. Jane found the magic formula for that."

Erick raised his head and looked at her for a long, searching moment. "I think her phrase was 'please don't go.' Stay in Thailand, Wendy, and marry me."

In answer she moved into his arms and raised her lips to his. He crushed her to him almost roughly and pressed his mouth to hers in the long, fulfilling kiss from which they had both held back too often. Waves of happiness spread through her, sweeping away all doubt and filling all the lonely corners of her heart.

Love—the way you want it!

Candlelight Romances

		TITLE NO.	
☐ A MAN OF HER CHOOSING by Nina Pykare $1.50		#554	(15133-3)
☐ PASSING FANCY by Mary Linn Roby $1.50		#555	(16770-1)
☐ THE DEMON COUNT by Anne Stuart $1.25		#557	(11906-5)
☐ WHERE SHADOWS LINGER by Janis Susan May $1.25		#556	(19777-5)
☐ OMEN FOR LOVE by Esther Boyd $1.25		#552	(16108-8)
☐ MAYBE TOMORROW by Marie Pershing $1.25		#553	(14909-6)
☐ LOVE IN DISGUISE by Nina Pykare $1.50		#548	(15229-1)
☐ THE RUNAWAY HEIRESS by Lillian Cheatham $1.50		#549	(18083-X)
☐ HOME TO THE HIGHLANDS by Jessica Eliot $1.25		#550	(13104-9)
☐ DARK LEGACY by Candace Connell $1.25		#551	(11771-2)
☐ LEGACY OF THE HEART by Lorena McCourtney $1.25		#546	(15645-9)
☐ THE SLEEPING HEIRESS by Phyllis Taylor Pianka $1.50		#543	(17551-8)
☐ DAISY by Jennie Tremaine $1.50		#542	(11683-X)
☐ RING THE BELL SOFTLY by Margaret James $1.25		#545	(17626-3)
☐ GUARDIAN OF INNOCENCE by Judy Boynton $1.25		#544	(11862-X)
☐ THE LONG ENCHANTMENT by Helen Nuelle $1.25		#540	(15407-3)
☐ SECRET LONGINGS by Nancy Kennedy $1.25		#541	(17609-3)

At your local bookstore or use this handy coupon for ordering:

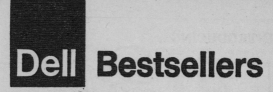

Dell Bestsellers